MINNIE

ANGEL CREEK CHRISTMAS BRIDES

SYLVIA MCDANIEL

Copyright

Copyright © 2020 Sylvia McDaniel
Published by Virtual Bookseller, LLC
All Rights Reserved
Cover Design: Dar Albert
Edited by Tina Winograd
Release date: November 2020
ebook ISBN 978-1-950858-37-8
Paperback ISBN 978-1-950858-38-5

This book and parts thereof may not be reproduced in any form, stored in a retrieval system, or transmitted in any form by any means—electronic, mechanical, photocopying, or otherwise—without prior written permission of the author and publisher, except as provided by the United States of America copyright law. The only exception is by a reviewer who may quote short excerpts in a review.

❀ Created with Vellum

Mail Order Bride With a Secret

Minnie Ravenel needs a husband now and an escape out of Charleston. Her mother answers an ad for a mail order bride in Angel Creek Montana, hoping that when Minnie arrives, the man will accept her and her unborn child.

Tripp Maddox isn't looking for a wife, but when he sees Minnie standing alone on the street crying, something about her situation reminds him of his own losses. A lonely rancher, with Christmas only a two months away, he asks her to marry him.

Can two desperate strangers make a life together or will the past tear them apart?

Sign up for my New Book Alert and receive a free book.

THE ANGEL CREEK CHRISTMAS BRIDES

After the war leaves Charleston devastated, and with few prospects of marriage, five friends headed west for a new life and a possible love match. A year later, they invite six friends to join them. The following Christmas, they're still homesick and in desperate need of a deeper connection with their old life, so what else can a Southern Belle do but invite more would-be brides to travel west?

Angel Creek is about to be invaded yet again by more Southern Misses and the town most definitely will never be the same!

CHRISTMAS 2018 BOOKS
Book 1: Charity — Sylvia McDaniel
Book 2: Julia — Lily Graison
Book 3: Ruby — Hildie McQueen
Book 4: Sarah — Peggy McKenzie
Book 5: Anna — Everly West

CHRISTMAS 2019 BOOKS
Book 6: Caroline — Lily Graison
Book 7: Melody — Caroline Clemmons
Book 8: Elizabeth — Jo Grafford
Book 9: Emma — Peggy McKenzie
Book 10: Viola — Cyndi Raye
Book 11: Ginger — Sylvia McDaniel

CHRISTMAS 2020 BOOKS
Book 12: Abigail — Peggy McKenzie
Book 13: Grace — Jo Grafford
Book 14: Pearl — Hildie McQueen
Book 15: Rebecca — Lily Graison
Book 16: Charlotte — Kari Trumbo
Book 17: Minnie — Sylvia McDaniel
Book 18: Adele — Cynthia Woolf
Book 19: Victoria — Maxine Douglas
Book 20: Meg — Caroline Clemmons

CHRISTMAS 2021 BOOKS
Book 21: Glenda — Hildie McQueen
Book 22: Temperance — Lily Graison
Book 23: Lilly — Jo Grafford
Book 24: Hannah — Peggy McKenzie
Book 25: Amy — Caroline Clemmons
Book 26: Cora — Sylvia McDaniel

CHAPTER 1

Christmas Eve 1888

Minnie Maddox tucked her children into bed, kissing them on the forehead, telling them each Merry Christmas.

Tonight was special. The night her beautiful brunette daughter turned eighteen. Minnie stared at her daughter, her heart swelling with love. The time had come to tell her the truth about her birth.

After they tucked the last child into bed, Minnie turned to her first born.

"There's something I want to talk to you about," she told her daughter.

For years, Minnie had dreaded this time and lay awake many nights knowing this day would someday arrive.

Her daughter looked confused.

"Come to bed and I will tell you the story of your birth."

She took her daughter's hand and led her into her bedroom. Once she was settled beneath the covers, Minnie crawled up beside her.

"Is this about Papa not being my real father?"

The girl knew. But how?

"He's your father in every sense of the word, but he did not create you. You see, he rescued me."

CHAPTER 2

October 1870 Angel Creek, Montana
"I'm going to town, Pops, do you want to go?" Tripp Maddox asked his father. The old man was sitting at the kitchen table eating lunch.

"We need a woman in this house who can cook," he said.

Pain ripped through Tripp's chest creating an ache near his heart. His sister, Beth, had been the cook of the family. After their mother died, she had taken over the housekeeping chores. But now she was gone too.

After a year, you would think the pain would go away.

"You should get married," he said.

A group of men in town had sent off for mail order brides and Tripp had considered ordering himself a wife, but decided he wasn't ready. Another woman coming in and taking her place, just made his heart hurt.

"Someday," he said, really not wanting to talk about this right now. He needed to get to town. "Do you want to go or not?"

The old man shook his head. "No, I'm missing your mother and Beth pretty fierce today."

Every day, it was the same and he didn't know if his father would ever get over the loss of his wife and daughter.

"Then come with me," Tripp said. "Being around people would do you some good."

At almost seventy, his father could be very stubborn.

His father shook her head. "Nope, I'm going out and say hello. Tell them I miss them."

Loyd went to the cemetery every week and Tripp went into town. He was not one to spend his time gazing at the graves remembering their loss.

Tripp missed his mother and his sister, Beth. The pain of her death slammed into him again, crushing his chest. The memory of her screaming in pain gave him nightmares. The expression on the doctor's face when he came out of her bedroom would always haunt him.

"Do you really think they hear you?"

"Don't matter, son. It makes me feel better. You go on into town. Be sure to bring me back some licorice. And if they have any baked goods in the mercantile, some cookies would be nice."

"Come get them yourself," he told his father, trying to encourage him to leave with him.

The man stood from the table. "Don't forget to get what I want."

It was his final command as he walked across the room, grabbed his jacket and hat and walked out the door. Soon Tripp heard his horse galloping down the lane.

"Stubborn old coot," he said out loud.

His mother had passed away suddenly about two years

ago, and then last year, his sister. It wasn't fair they both died so close together. He'd barely gotten over losing his mother when the problems with Beth started.

With a sigh, he grabbed his coat and hat and walked out the door. It took him a few minutes to hitch the wagon and then he was on the road.

An hour later, he arrived in Angel Creek. The bustling small town had one main road where all the businesses were located. The town was growing with the nearby Fort Benton, the mines, and cattle ranches.

He pulled into the parking area for the mercantile, then jumped out of his wagon.

The stagecoach had just pulled in and he heard the driver calling out, "Angel Creek, Montana."

In this spot, many men in town had found their woman, their wife. In this place, mail order brides met their soon-to-be husbands. It was a place that often drew Tripp as he watched couples embrace for the first time.

The stage driver jumped down and pulled out a step stool before he opened the door.

Tripp stared as a beautiful brunette descended the stairs of the stagecoach. Mesmerized by the gorgeous pregnant woman, a warmth filled his chest. She was already some lucky man's wife, but why was she traveling to Angel Creek? Especially right before winter set in.

Robert Larsen stood before the stage, glancing around. A heartless man, no one in town approved of his cold, ignorant ways. It wasn't that he couldn't be kind, but he was gruff and mean and Tripp hoped he wasn't who was waiting for this woman.

"What happened to Miss Ravenel?" he asked the woman.

Unable to stop himself, Tripp's feet seemed to move of their own accord as he crossed the street. Something drew him to her. For some reason, she needed his protection.

"I'm Minnie Ravenel," she said.

Robert's face turned red and his fist clinched, and for a moment, Tripp feared he would hit the woman.

Voice raised, he yelled at her. "No, you're pregnant. You're supposed to be a virgin. Some man has already planted a babe in your belly."

Tripp watched the woman recoil like he'd slapped her. She stood there not responding while Robert's voice grew louder and louder. If it was his intent to shame the woman, he was doing a fine job.

"No woman of mine is going to be a loose, sinful woman."

Tears begin to roll down her cheeks as she hung her head in obvious distress. This couldn't be good for the baby or her.

"You should have told me," Robert shouted. "I would have told you to stay home. I'm never marrying a pregnant slut."

The stagecoach driver placed her trunk at her feet and then stayed close by.

Robert glanced one last time at the woman, spit at her feet. "Whore. Go back home."

She seemed to almost crumble as tears rolled down her cheeks and she lowered her head in shame.

Rage consumed Tripp as he hurried toward the sobbing woman.

Robert walked away as Tripp approached her. It was all he could do not to go after the man and punch him. But that would only draw more attention to the poor woman as a crowd begin to gather on the street.

"Are you all right?" he asked her.

Her head lifted and she gazed at him with the most beautiful emerald eyes that reminded him of spring grasses, sparkling with tears.

"No," she said. "Is there a hotel where I can stay until the next stage leaves?"

The driver set another bag near her trunk. "Lady, you're on the last stage until next spring."

Her legs began to buckle and Tripp reached out to keep her from falling. Like a hammer to his heart, he knew immediately what he had to do. He had no other choice as he was unable to walk away from her.

"Look at me," he whispered. "It's going to be all right."

"How can you say that? You're not pregnant and unmarried. My mother wrote him. I thought she told him I was expecting."

Relief filled Tripp that she had not misled Robert by keeping her pregnancy from him. But how could a mother do this to her pregnant daughter?

Tripp smiled. "To be honest, you just got real lucky that you're not getting hitched to Robert Larsen."

A certainty filled him. Whoever this woman was, something about her attracted him. Something made him want to protect her. He wanted to marry her.

With his heart thumping wildly, he grabbed her hand and dropped to one knee. "Marry me instead."

He wasn't certain of her name, but he was offering to be her husband and spend the rest of his life with her. What the hell was he doing?

Maybe he was crazy, but it felt right. If she agreed to marry him, he would be the luckiest man alive.

"You don't know me," she said.

"Did you know Robert Larsen?"

A smile crossed her face. "No."

"Look, you need a husband and I need a wife. My papa was telling me just today that I should get married. And you stepped off the stage and I thought some man was lucky to have you as his wife."

Her eyes widened. "Really? You thought that?"

"Yes, I did."

Still on his knees, he gazed into the most gorgeous eyes with long black lashes. "So is that a yes or a no?"

"Yes," she said. "I'm Minnie Ravenel."

He grinned and rose to his feet. "Tripp Maddox. Welcome to Angel Creek."

The stagecoach driver who had been standing off to the side started clapping. "Congratulations, you two."

"Thank you," Tripp said, a sense of unrealness coming over him. "I'll get the wagon and we can load her trunks. Need to stop by the mercantile and pick up some supplies. Then we'll head to the church."

Minnie stood to the side, a shy smile on her beautiful face. The memory of Beth overwhelmed him. She would be so proud of him today.

CHAPTER 3

Minnie walked beside Tripp through the frontier town—beautiful with pine and maple trees, but so different from her hometown of Charleston. And colder.

Sliding her eyes over to the man who had just asked her to marry him, warmth and nerves rattled her. The man was so strong and handsome that he took her breath away.

So much better than the man who rejected her.

Dark hair and a straight nose, high cheekbones, dark lashes that framed his sparkly blue eyes that twinkled. Full lips that she suddenly realized would soon be kissing her.

Nerves shivered through her and she started shaking.

"Are you cold?"

"No," she said, licking her lips as she gazed at him, wondering what she should tell him.

Suddenly the enormity of what she was about to do slammed into her and she stopped. They were outside a tall white building, the church, where they were going to be married.

Was she crazy? But what choice did she have?

"Wait," she said, placing her hand on her chest, feeling her rapidly beating heart.

"Are you all right?"

"Why are you doing this? Why are you marrying me?"

Tripp smiled, took her hand and kissed the back of it. "When I saw you step out of the stagecoach, I was enthralled with your beauty."

"But I'm pregnant with another man's child. How will you treat the baby once it's born?"

It was a fear she had carried since she got on the train in Charleston. What man would want to raise another man's child?

"Once we're married, that baby is mine," he said. "I will love it and treat it like it's one of my own and it will be, unless you think the father will come after you."

Richard would never want this baby or her, so she had no fear of him coming after her. In fact, she hoped she never saw him again.

"No, you don't have to worry about him coming after me or the baby."

Tripp smiled. "Any other questions or problems you want to discuss before we get hitched?"

"It's just I don't know you."

"And I don't know you either, but standing there watching you, something told me you were mine. Something said marry you, that's your wife."

"Really?"

"Really," he said, smiling down at her. He leaned forward and kissed her lightly on the lips.

Heat spread through her. And for a moment, she couldn't

believe that fate was being so kind. Tripp seemed like a nice man.

"We'll take things slow and get to know each other," he said. "If you decide I'm not the man for you, then let me know and I'll put you back on the stage in the spring and you can return to Charleston."

She tilted her head and gazed at him. Why was he being so generous?

"My only other question is why hasn't a nice man like you been snatched up?"

He laughed. "Look around. Angel Creek is a beautiful little mountain town, but single women are scarce. I'd say about seventy-five percent of the women were once mail order brides just like yourself."

That was incredible. She couldn't help but wonder if any of them had been pregnant when they arrived. Almost seven months pregnant.

"When word got out that Robert didn't want you, you would have had a string of men outside your door waiting to ask you to marry them. It was my lucky day and I found you before everyone else."

The town was beautiful with the streets busy with wagons rumbling down Main Street. Businesses on every corner, people strolling down the wooden sidewalks. If snow arrived, it would be beautiful.

"Does it snow here?"

He nodded. "All winter."

"Oh, I can't wait to see snow. It rains in Charleston, but it never snows."

They stood there for a few more minutes, gazing at one

another. "Are your nerves settled? Are you ready to get married now?"

She didn't know Tripp, but he seemed like a nice man and as long as he would accept her and the baby, then she would marry him.

"Yes, let's get married," she said, taking a deep breath to calm her rapidly beating heart.

With a smile, Tripp opened the door and waited for her to enter the church. Inside was an entryway with wooden floors. The chapel had rough-hewn pews with a cross hanging in the front. The simple setting was beautiful and smelled of incense.

Would the preacher marry them with her so big and pregnant?

"Flint, are you here?" he called.

A tall dark haired man and a small petite woman with red hair came around the corner. The woman's belly was rounded with pregnancy.

She hurried to her. "You're expecting. Congratulations."

Tears welled up in Minnie's eyes. No one had told her congratulations or been happy for her. And yet this stranger who didn't know her situation welcomed her.

"Thank you," she said.

"Tripp good to see you. What can I do for you?" the preacher asked.

"I'm Ginger Carroll and this is my husband Flint," the pregnant woman said. "Did you come from Charleston?"

"Yes," Minnie said stunned.

"Tripp good to see you. What can I do for you?" the preacher asked.

"We want to get married," he said. "Minnie just arrived on the stage and I asked her to marry me."

Ginger smiled at Tripp and then glanced at Minnie. "That's wonderful. How far along are you?"

"Almost seven months," Minnie said, feeling like the woman was not a stranger but a good friend.

"I'm Ginger Carroll and this is my husband Flint," she said. "Did you come from Charleston?"

"Yes," Minnie said.

"Me too. I came here because my friends had come as mail order brides and found husbands. There were no eligible men in Charleston at the time."

Minnie's heart squeezed with pain. If only she had done something similar instead of believing in Richard's promises and lies.

"I can't imagine making that trip expecting," Ginger said. "You must be exhausted."

The trip had worn her out and she knew that once they reached Tripp's home, she would probably collapse into the bed. Just then the baby kicked, and she reached down and patted her tummy.

"How far along are you?" Minnie asked.

"Oh, I'm due in about two weeks. In fact, I wish this little one would make his or her appearance, so I could see my toes once again."

Minnie realized that soon, she would be that big and she glanced at her soon-to-be husband. How would he feel with her so big and unable to do much? Would he accept her?

Flint frowned at the two women. "Tripp, are you certain this is what you want?"

"Absolutely," he said, glancing at Minnie. "I want her for my wife and the baby will be my child."

Ginger grinned at him. "Minnie, you are a very lucky woman. Tripp is a good man."

Her heart filled with hope. For the last seven months, she'd felt so abandoned, worthless, and already her soon-to-be husband was making her feel better.

A stranger, yet he wanted her and the baby. Already he'd protected her and he seemed like a good man.

The preacher gazed at Minnie. "No jilted lover is going to follow you to Angel Creek?"

If only the man knew. Richard was not a jilted lover and his family would be mortified if he came after her.

"No, never," she said. She would shoot him, if he did.

"Then let's get you two married," Flint said. "Sorry for the awkward questions, but I want the couples I marry to consider everything before they agree to spend their lives together."

Minnie understood, but she'd already suffered enough humiliation all because a man ignored her when she said no.

"Come with me and we'll get you all freshened up and then you can marry that handsome man," Ginger said, taking her by the hand.

Minnie glanced back at Tripp and he smiled. They were about to say *I do*. This handsome man was about to become her husband and the baby's father.

CHAPTER 4

The wedding was over. They were officially man and wife as the preacher and his wife threw rice over them as they left the church.

It had been a beautiful ceremony. Private with just the four of them and Ginger had lent her a veil and gloves. Afterward, she served them a slice of cake she had just baked and Minnie was grateful. She'd been starving.

Tripp helped her up into the wagon for the ride to his home, which she hadn't even thought to ask him about. What if he lived in a shack?

It didn't matter as long as he cared for her and the baby.

"Bye," Ginger called. "Good luck with your pregnancy and your marriage."

"Thank you," Minnie said as she sat on the bench in the wagon. A hard surface that she hoped would not be a rough ride to his home.

Tripp climbed in and released the brake and called to the horses. Soon they were on their way.

"How far is your home?" Minnie asked.

"The ranch is about an hour from town. Next week, I think we should come back to town and get you a few winter items you're going to need. Also have the doctor take a look at you."

She hung her head. No doctor had helped her with her pregnancy. Her mother had taken her, but he refused to see her because she was unmarried and she had created such a scene at the wedding.

As far as he was concerned, it would be better if her baby died. It would be better if she died.

Rubbing her hand over her stomach, she felt protective. It was not this child's fault that her father didn't want her or the baby. All she prayed for was a safe delivery and that Tripp would keep his word and love the child.

"Are you all right?"

"I'm tired, so I'm glad we're heading to your home. Seeing a doctor is a good idea, if he will accept me."

The man looked at her, confused. "Of course, he will."

"No, the doctor in Charleston refused to see me."

Tripp's face tensed and he turned to her. "You're no longer in Charleston. People are not like that here."

She hoped he was right. The moment she announced her pregnancy, hoping to save the bride and also show the world that Richard was not a good man, friends and family had turned their back on her. She was on her own.

During her time in Charleston, she'd been shocked by how many people wanted nothing to do with an unwed mother.

So far, Tripp had been kind and generous and more than she expected in a husband, but what were his flaws?

"Tell me about yourself. About your ranch. You know I'm a city girl and have never lived outside Charleston."

He didn't glance at her but kept his eyes on the horses and the road ahead. The sun was getting low in the sky and Minnie was so ready to reach her final destination.

"I'm twenty-six years old, the oldest and now the only child of my parents. My mother and sister have passed away, so it's just been my father and me for the last year. Pops is an older man who has been after me to get married for quite some time. So you're going to make him very happy."

She smiled. Her own father died in the Civil War, so it would be nice to have a father figure around again, if he accepted her. Even though Tripp said he would, there was always the chance he wouldn't want a pregnant daughter-in-law.

"Together, the two of us herd the cattle, work the horses, feed the chickens, and take turns cooking. His is better than mine. Do you know how to cook?"

Minnie bit her bottom lip. They had servants and she'd never taken an interest. In fact, looking back on her life, what had she learned to do besides make perfect table arrangements, host lavish dinner parties and be the perfect social wife? All totally useless here in Montana.

"No, I'm sorry. We had servants who cooked the meals."

He laughed. "You're going to be in for quite a shock. You'll be in charge of the house, the cooking and cleaning. And probably gathering the eggs."

Taking a deep breath, she knew she had to prepare herself for a new life. One without the luxuries of her home, but that didn't bother her as long as he was patient while she learned.

The sun reflected off the snow-topped mountains and she

gasped at the beautiful sight. Montana was gorgeous in a rugged kind of way and her new life sounded like it would be completely different from what she was used to.

"I'll do my best to learn," she promised, knowing she had to contribute something. Especially after everything that Tripp had done for her.

She liked the looks of her rugged husband. A cowboy hat sat on his head, his hands looked worn, his arms strong and his thighs thick and muscular.

"What about you? Did you have family back home?"

"My mother and sister. Mother wanted me gone from Charleston, so I didn't ruin my sister Nora's chance of catching a husband."

A frown crossed his face. "Didn't that hurt you?"

"Yes and no. I was in such a state of shock that nothing much penetrated until she packed me up and put me on the train to St. Louis. Then I felt so lonely."

He reached over and grabbed her hand and squeezed it. "You're not going to be lonely anymore."

Warmth filled her at his words as she gazed at the pine trees lining the road. It was beautiful here in a rugged kind of way. "Tell me what you expect from your wife."

With a sigh, he smiled. "Just a loving woman who will give me children, comfort me when I'm sad, and be by my side. I know we don't know each other and you've had a long journey. We'll take things slow."

The wagon hit a hole in the road and she bounced on the seat, her tired and sore rear end coming down hard. "That's all?"

"What more could a man want? My parents had a happy

marriage and that's all I want. I hope that eventually you'll fall in love with me."

She thought about that for a moment. As long as they continued on the path they were on, she could see that being a very strong possibility. As long as he fought for and loved her and the baby.

"What do you want in a husband?"

"Someone who puts me first. Who loves me and cherishes me and tries to make me happy. Someone who will stand by me and not desert me in the bad times. Someone who accepts this child."

"You got it," he said, smiling at her.

"Is there anything about you I should know?"

He thought for a moment. "Sometimes I'm moody. Sometimes I can get cranky and withdrawn. It's not that I mean to, but there is something on my mind. What about you?"

What could she say? That right now she was an emotional wreck being pregnant. She had shed more tears in the last few months over the simplest of things. And yet Richard's deception had left her more angry than hurt.

"I'm very emotional, right now. More than I've ever been in my entire life. I cry at the least little thing, so be patient with me."

"Beth was the same way," he said.

"Who's Beth?"

"My sister," he said, his face closing off.

"The one who died?"

"Yes," he said. "Look the road to the house is ahead. We're almost home."

Why did she have the feeling that he suddenly changed the

subject? And was his sister pregnant when she died? He said she was the same way.

As they turned up the lane, Minnie stared at the house ahead. A log home with smoke curling up out of the chimney, with a big wraparound porch.

Her new home. Her new life.

CHAPTER 5

The sun was sinking behind the mountains when the wagon turned up the lane. Minnie watched as an older man walked out onto the porch and gazed at her like was seeing a ghost. He must be Tripp's father, her new father-in-law.

The gentleman stood on the porch, his expression confused. His appearance was an older version of Tripp, and Minnie knew how her husband would look when he aged.

Slowly, Tripp pulled the wagon to a halt. He jumped down and hurried to help Minnie from the wagon.

"Pops, come meet my bride."

"What? You got married? When did you plan this?"

"I didn't. It just happened."

The man stepped down the stairs from the wooden porch, gazing at Minnie like he couldn't believe what he was seeing.

"You've been telling me to find a wife and today I did," Tripp said with a grin.

He lifted Minnie from the wagon and then walked her to

his father. "Minnie, this is my father, Loyd Maddox, otherwise known as Pops."

"Good to meet you, sir," she said, holding out her hand.

"You too, Minnie. Please forgive me, I'm a little shocked."

She smiled. "I understand, sir."

"Where did you meet my son?"

"Today at the stagecoach."

"An unusual meet, but you're as pretty as a peach orchard in spring. Forgive me, you must be exhausted. Come into the house and sit a spell while Tripp carries everything in and puts the wagon up. You can tell me why you decided to marry my son."

"Thanks, Pops. You could help me."

"Nope, I'm going to meet my new daughter-in-law."

With a grin, Tripp walked back to the wagon and began to unload the supplies and her trunks.

"Call me Pops. That's the name my children gave me."

"Yes, sir," she said.

"Come in, my dear. Sit and I'll get you a hot cup of tea," he said. "The weather is changing, and the evenings are getting downright cold. We should have snow falling any day now."

That sounded heavenly as Minnie walked into the house. Her first impression was simple and homey. A big fireplace was centered on a wall and she could feel the welcome heat from the flames filling the room.

"You'll soon learn to bundle up when the sun starts going down. Sit anywhere you like. I'll be back."

A nearby rocker looked inviting and she sank down in the chair close to the fireplace. Their home was a mixture of handmade throws and a horsehair sofa with matching end tables and pictures of family. The room had oil lamps that needed to be lit as darkness approached.

The man walked into a kitchen area and hung a kettle over the separate fireplace. The hot tea would warm her chilled bones. After warm Charleston, Montana would take some getting used to.

When he came back, he carried a cup of steaming tea.

"I hope you don't mind, but I put a little honey in to sweeten it up."

"Thank you," she said, letting the hot mug warm her hands.

"My wife loved to sit in that very chair, knitting or reading in the evenings. God love the woman, I still miss her."

"I'm sorry. How long has it been?"

"Two years," he said. "She had been waiting for this day. Longing for another daughter and grandbabies."

Minnie licked her lips as she waited for the tea to cool. Tripp came in and out, delivering boxes of goodies. Things they picked up at the mercantile.

"So tell me how you met my son," he said.

She gave him an abbreviated version of what happened to her today and how Robert had backed out of marrying her.

The older man shook his head. "You don't want anything to do with Robert Larsen. He's not a good man."

"That's what Tripp said."

The man looked kind of perplexed as he stared at her. "What did your family think of you coming to Montana?"

Her mother couldn't wait to get her out of the house. If only she had asked how she had gotten pregnant, but she never did. She assumed her daughter let Richard have his way with her. She was wrong. The anger still ate at Minnie, but nothing would ever change the way her mother reacted.

"My mother was the one who corresponded with Robert. And in his defense, I don't think she mentioned I was pregnant. So he was understandably upset when I showed up."

The man shook his head. "He's not the type of man to accept the unexpected."

She sighed and gave a smile. "Tripp walked right over after he left and offered to marry me. We went to the mercantile and then to the church. The preacher and his wife Ginger were so wonderful when they married us," she said. "Really nice people."

Pops nodded. "Yes, Mrs. Carroll is expecting her first child as well. How far along are you?"

Why did she feel uncomfortable talking to this man and what must he think of her marrying his son while pregnant with another man's child?

"Almost seven months. Tripp mentioned we should go to the doctor next week and have him check me out."

The man stood and walked to the fireplace. "Welcome to the family, Minnie. It's been over a year since we've had a woman in the house, so you'll have to excuse the mess. We're just a couple of bachelors living here."

She glanced down and shook her head. "I'm not very domesticated."

The man pulled back. "What do you mean?"

"I don't know how to cook or clean or anything. We had servants to prepare the meals and clean the house."

Why did she feel ashamed of the fact that before the war, her father made enough money for them to live comfortably? Enough money that when he died, they didn't have to worry about what would happen. Of course, as a banker, he did not convert his cash into confederacy money, calling that a ludicrous idea.

Like betting in a gambling hall.

Instead, he went to war for the North, keeping his opinions to himself as he fought the South, living in one of their cities.

He laughed. "Oh, honey, you're going to get a real education. I'll help you learn how to cook and do my best with teaching you to clean. The laundry is the hardest. Especially in the winter."

Minnie had never done laundry and certainly not in the cold. But she would learn.

"Thank you, I want to be a good wife to Tripp and not a burden."

"Let me give you some sage advice. Marriage is not all hearts and flowers. It's hard work. Women have one idea of marriage and men another. Somewhere in the middle is where you have to meet. Never forget your husband and family are more important than anything or anyone else. Mainly, love my son and be his help mate."

"I'll do my best," she said, thinking this was not just for a night or a week, but a lifetime. And right now, she knew nothing about her husband, but she would learn.

"Now, I'm going to go fix tonight's supper, because frankly you don't want to eat Tripp's cooking on your first night here."

Tripp walked in with her trunk. "Hey, I heard that."

"Tomorrow if you're rested, I'll start to teach you how to cook. I'm not a great cook, but we'll start with the basics."

Minnie was so tired, she would have preferred to go

straight to bed, but the baby needed food and nourishment. She would eat and then excuse herself.

It was their wedding night and while Tripp promised they would wait, she still felt uneasy. She'd never shared a bed with a man. Never lived in the same room. This would be a whole new way of life.

"I can set a beautiful table," she said to his father.

Pops laughed. "You society girls are always good for that sort of thing. But out here in the west, we're doing good to use a napkin."

A smile crossed her face. "I think I have a lot to learn."

"Oh yes, you sure do."

At least Tripp's home seemed happy. Not the tomb hers had become when her mother learned of her pregnancy.

CHAPTER 6

After dinner, Minnie excused herself and went to bed. His new wife was exhausted and could barely keep her eyes open.

"Do you need any help," he asked as she stood from the table.

"No, thank you, though I would love a bath tomorrow evening," she said.

"That can be arranged," he said. "Get some rest. I'll be in later."

"Good night, Pops," she said.

"Good night, Minnie," he replied as the men watched her go into the bedroom.

They started stacking the dishes, carrying them into the kitchen like they did every night. But tonight there was a tenseness in the air.

While they heated the water, his father stood, arms crossed.

"Go ahead and say what's on your mind," Tripp said,

knowing his father. He didn't care. In his heart, he was certain he had made a good decision.

"Minnie is not your sister," he said. "Are you certain about this?"

"Thank God, she's not my sister. Someday I hope to sleep with her."

Tripp laughed at the expression on his father's stunned face.

"You know what I mean. You married her because she reminds you of Beth."

Tripp thought about what his father was saying. He would have helped Beth in any way possible, but he didn't see Beth when he saw Minnie.

No, he saw a gorgeous woman in trouble. One that with just a glance, he felt drawn to.

"No, I swear to you, Pops, when she stepped off that stagecoach, it was like lightning struck me. And that was before Robert was so ruthless to her."

He began to wash the dishes, his father drying them as they worked side by side in the kitchen like normal.

"But when she started crying, I couldn't reach her fast enough. Sure, the pregnancy reminds me of Beth, but the woman I wanted for my wife."

When Minnie felt comfortable, he hoped she would tell him about the baby's father and what happened. But he was not going to pressure her. It didn't matter. All that mattered was that she was his wife and this baby would be his.

"It was that way with your mother," Pops said, drying a plate and stacking it in the cabinet. "One glance and I was a complete fool for her."

"Really? You and mother were love at first sight?"

His parents had a loving marriage and he hoped that eventually he and Minnie would have the same. The fact that his father was struck when he saw his mother gave him hope.

"Yes, but I courted her for a number of months before I asked her father for her hand in marriage."

"We didn't have the time," he said. "There's a baby coming and that child is going to have my name."

For a moment, there was silence in the kitchen as one washed and the other dried. It was a routine and yet the men were comfortable doing the dishes.

"Do you know anything about the father?"

Tripp had felt relief when Flint asked her about the father of her child. And she had answered him very quickly and resoundingly.

"No, she's not told me anything except that I have no worries about the man following her to try to take her back."

Tripp hoped and prayed that was true, but if the situation were reversed, he'd follow her to the ends of the earth to bring her home. Married or not.

"Take it slow, son," his father said. "She's been hurt. And ole Robert didn't exactly make her feel any better about her situation."

The urge to find Robert was strong. To plant his fists in his face, but he needed to let it go. The man was the worst.

"Dad, she was weeping. There was no way I could walk away from a pregnant woman with no place to go. And oddly enough, I didn't want to."

They finished chores then walked into the living room. His father pulled out the whiskey bottle and poured them each a drink.

"To you and Minnie, may you have a long happy marriage,"

he said. "Your mother would've been so happy and proud of what you did today."

Tripp smiled. Yes, it seemed like he'd been a good Samaritan and he wished he could feel that way, but he wanted Minnie in the worst possible way. Even with her body rounded with child, when she gazed at him with her emerald eyes and dark lashes, all he wanted was to pick her up and carry her into the bedroom.

They clinked their glasses together and downed the shot of whiskey that went down and warmed his chest.

"Thanks, Pops," he said.

Sitting in front of the fire, they were silent for a few moments before his father turned to him. "Are you all right raising another man's child?"

"Of course. In fact, she asked me before we were married. I told her that child is mine now that we're married, and I will treat it as such."

His father nodded. "Good. It's no one's business."

"No," Tripp said. "Think of how some of the town people treated Beth. I would be so upset if anyone treated Minnie wrong. In fact, they might be meeting my fists if I find out."

They sat there and watched the flames flicker and the wood pop and sizzle in the fireplace.

"A child in the house. It's been so long since you and your sister were little. It will be trying and wonderful at the same time."

"Trying?"

His father laughed. "Just wait until those midnight feedings or when the little one will not go to sleep. Oh, your mother would have so enjoyed being here now."

Tripp's heart ached at the thought of his mother. She

wanted grandchildren so badly, but death took her before she received her wish.

"I know, Pops, but I hope she knows we're thinking of her," he said to try to comfort his father.

The older man stood. "Time for bed. We've both got an early morning tomorrow. Let your wife sleep tonight."

Tripp grinned. "I will. Get some rest."

"You too. Don't know if I'm going to let you go to town alone anymore. Send you for supplies and you came back with a wife."

He watched his father disappear into his bedroom. Tripp sat, watching the fire a little longer. Today, he'd taken on a lot of responsibility and yet, he felt so good about his decision.

Finally, he stood and went into the bedroom. In the dim light, he could see Minnie curled beneath the sheets as far on her side as she could get.

A warm feeling filled him as he stared down at her and began to unbutton his shirt. He slipped off his shirt and pants and then slipped into bed beside her wearing nothing but his long johns.

While he knew that nothing would happen tonight, he couldn't resist holding her. He slipped his arm beneath her and she moaned.

"Go back to sleep, Minnie," he whispered and kissed her on the cheek.

The smell of lavender filled his nose as he held his wife. It was going to be a long night as his manhood swelled at the feel of his wife's silken skin.

It would take time, but he couldn't wait until he took her and made her his.

CHAPTER 7

The next morning, Minnie woke to an empty bed. Last night, she dreamed that Tripp crawled in bed beside her and held her during the night. And yet it didn't feel like a dream, but real.

This morning, the sun was shining and she feared she had overslept. When she got out of bed, she went to the wash basin and quickly splashed her face with the cold water.

She could see her breath in the room and knew it had to be cold. Opening her trunk, she looked through her dresses and realized none of them would keep her warm.

After donning her only other dress that the waist didn't cinch her in, she opened the door and saw no one in the living room. Going into the kitchen, she gazed about the room. Very soon she would be the one cooking. She gazed at the utensils and had no idea what they did.

She found the bread and butter and heated it over the flame, burning one side.

They expected her to cook?

A quick glance at her watch pendant let her know it was

after nine. She had slept well over twelve hours. But today, she felt rested, refreshed even.

The fresh bread, even burned, tasted delicious.

"Good morning," Tripp said, walking into the room. She jumped. "Sorry, I didn't mean to scare you. How are you feeling?"

"Better. A good night's sleep is good. It's been a long time since I wasn't moving."

He walked up behind her and put his arms around her and kissed her on the cheek. This morning, he smelled of the outdoors. A sweet woodsy scent.

"If you feel like it, I thought that today we could go for a ride around the place. I could show you the mountains and rolling plains."

While she was tired of jostling about in the wagon, she did want to see the ranch and the place where she would be living. She had never been on a ranch before.

She turned in his arms and gazed up into his sky-blue eyes. "I would like that."

"If you're tired of being in a wagon, we can wait, but I promise you we won't go far," he said.

It was considerate of him to think about how tired she was of being on the move, but she was curious about where she was living. And if they waited too much longer, the weather or her condition could stop her from seeing the property.

"Do you have a coat I can wear? It's rather chilly here and my clothes are lighter."

Quickly she was learning that she would need to make some winter clothes. But not until after the baby arrived. Right now, her expanding waistline did not need new dresses.

He grinned. "When we go to town, we're going to take care of that. You're going to need boots and heavy winter woolies."

"Woolies?"

"Yes, like thick socks, long johns and a heavy-duty coat."

"Women don't wear long johns," she told him with a grin.

"Maybe not in South Carolina, but Angel Creek, Montana, the temperature says put on anything that will keep you warm."

It was such a strange life here and she hoped she would adjust to the different weather.

"All right, let me put on a heavier slip and then I'll meet you outside. Should we take a picnic lunch? I'm sorry I slept so late this morning."

He reached out and brushed a curl away from her face. "You were tired. I'm glad you slept in. I'll meet you outside and I'll have a big coat for you to wear."

With a grin, she finished her toast and then hurried into the bedroom where she added a heavier layer of wool beneath her skirt. The baby kicked her letting her know he or she approved of the warmer clothing.

A smile spread across her face and she reached down and rubbed her belly. "Hello, little one, we're home and you're going to have a good papa."

At least, she hoped and prayed that Tripp's word was good and that he would accept her child. After Richard, she had a hard time trusting a man's word.

Eager to see her husband, she hurried out the door as fast as an expectant mother could.

Tripp stood waiting for her, picnic basket in hand. A blanket for her to wrap up in the wagon and a heavy coat were in his other hand and he held the coat for her to slide her arms in. Then he helped her into the wagon and wrapped the lap blanket around her. "I made us a lunch, but it's mainly some ham and cheese and an apple."

"That's perfect," she said, knowing she would be starving shortly. But that was all right.

Pops came out of the barn and smiled at them. "You kids have fun. I'll have dinner ready when you get back. Tripp don't be gone too long. That baby is going to get tired of being bounced around in that wagon."

"Yes, Pops," he said as he released the brake and clicked to the horses.

"Are you warm enough?"

"Oh yes," she said. "Your father is nice."

"He's an ornery old coot, but I think he's happy I married."

She smiled.

"How many acres do you own?"

"Right now, ten thousand. We're one of the largest ranches in the area. Pops bought as much land as he could afford when he and mother moved out here over twenty years ago. I was just a small tyke at the time."

The wagon bounced and Minnie grabbed the side.

"Sorry, I didn't see that hole. If you get tired, let me know and we'll go home."

She didn't want to go back to the house yet. She wanted to spend time with her husband, get to know him. They had not been married even twenty-four hours and she knew so little about this man who rescued her.

"I'm fine," she told him, gazing out at the landscape. A mountains of pine trees were on one side and the other was rolling hills of grass.

Cattle mooed in the distance and the smell of manure reached her nose. "They are smelly."

He laughed. "Yes, and over in that far pasture is where we keep the horses. Of course, now that winter is just weeks away, we'll be moving everything closer to the house."

"You need to teach me to be a rancher's wife," she said with a grin.

"Darling, I can't wait," he said smiling. "When spring comes, that's our busiest time. Calving season, cattle drives, mending fences, we stay busy."

Never in her life had she thought of herself moving to a cattle ranch, but here she was, and frankly, she felt eager about learning this new life.

He pulled the wagon to a halt beneath a lone tree. "I wanted to bring you here. This is the family tree. My mother and father carved their initials in the trunk and if you don't object, I'd like to carve ours as well."

A big smile spread across her face. No man had ever done that with her. Never. "I'd love to. What a neat idea."

Tripp came around to the side of the wagon and lifted her out. His hands slid down her arms and he pulled her in close.

His lips crashed down on hers as his mouth ravaged hers. It was as if he wanted to consume her lips as his mouth ravished hers. No man had ever kissed her like this as heat flooded her body and she moaned as he held her face in place.

Desire sweep down her spine to her center and she groaned. If this was how he kissed, what would it be like when he made love to her. Because this time, she would not accept anything less than a man making love to her.

When he released her, he smiled down at her. "I've wanted

to kiss you like that for a while, but the time hasn't been right."

A blush spread across her face. "That Tripp was a kiss unlike anything I've ever experienced."

"Good?"

"Definitely," she whispered, staring up into his blue eyes.

"Great, let's continue the tradition," he said, taking her hand and placing it on his arm.

They walked to the tree and suddenly he froze. His hand reached out and he studied the initials. She could see the despair in his eyes.

"What's wrong?"

"That's my sister Beth's initials along with someone else. Someone I don't recognize," he said frowning.

"Was she married?"

"No," he said in a voice she didn't recognize.

"A suitor?"

"No man in her life that we knew," he said. "But there was someone."

Anger etched his features and she could see his blue eyes glare with hate.

"If I find that man, I'll kill him."

Minnie stood in shock staring at her husband. What had this man done to Beth? Why would her husband want to kill him?

CHAPTER 8

Tripp tried to be easy going and attentive to Minnie, but after seeing the initials, GBH, he'd been stunned. Was this the mystery man who had gotten his sister pregnant and disappeared. Who hadn't been around to watch her grow large with his child? Who never married her? Who wasn't by her side when she and the baby died?

He clenched his fists, his anger rising inside him, gripping his chest in a way that made him want to roar his frustration. Beth was his only sibling. Tears welled up in his eyes.

Oh, how he missed her even a year later.

It was late afternoon when the wagon rolled back in front of the house. He knew the afternoon had not gone as well as he planned because of his anger at seeing the initials.

Even when he talked, his voice had been stilted. His mind racing with who they knew with the letters GBH.

He ruined the day. Setting the brake, he jumped out of the wagon and went around to his wife.

When he helped Minnie out of the wagon, he held her for

a moment. "I'm sorry. The initials on the tree took me by surprise."

She glanced up at him and he could see the concern in her gaze. "It's all right. I don't understand what's going on. You've told me Beth was your sister. Yet you're so angry at GBH. Someday I hope you'll tell me about her life and what happened to her."

With that, she turned and walked away. His chest ached. He disappointed his wife and it was his fault.

How could he tell a pregnant woman how his sister died in childbirth? Why frighten Minnie when he was suddenly scared enough for both of them?

Damn, he'd made a mess of things. But seeing Beth's initials with a man's reminded him of how he had let her down. He was her brother and he should have protected her from a scalawag who didn't love her enough to marry her.

Climbing back up in the wagon, he drove it into the barn where he unhitched the horses and rubbed them down. When he was irritated, this simple task let him think and ease his pain.

Thirty minutes later, his father walked into the barn.

"From Minnie's expression, it would appear things didn't go well. What happened?"

"Who has the initials GBH?"

His father frowned at him. "How the hell would I know?"

"Right below yours and mother's initials, Beth's were carved into the tree with GBH."

A deep sigh escaped from his father. "I haven't been up to that old tree in quite some time. Years in fact, so I haven't seen them. That must be the father of her child."

"Exactly," Tripp said. "Seeing that was like a slap to the

face. It brought back all the times we tried to get her to tell us who the father was."

His father sank down on a milking stool. "One thing about Beth, she was as stubborn as your mother."

Tripp glanced at his father. "And you're not stubborn?"

The old man's brows raised, his eyes growing large like Tripp had just insulted him.

"Of course, I am, but not in a womanly way," he said. "Beth and your mother, when they got mad, they could damn near freeze a man out. You'd best learn to pay attention to your woman unless you want to receive this treatment."

Tripp continued to brush the horse, the mare making little soothing noises. "When we got home, I apologized to her. Not that it made her feel any better. But seeing those initials, all I could think about was where and who this coward is."

His father shook his head at him. "Son, Beth has been gone for over a year. Nothing is going to bring her back. Even if you learned who the man is, what can you do? Punch him? Kill him? All that will do is get you into trouble."

What his father said was true, but the urge to defend his sister's reputation, even in death, was strong. Why did he leave her and his child?

"You've got a beautiful, pregnant wife in the house who you need to be courting. If you want this marriage to work, you have to show and prove to her that you didn't marry her just to clean house. Women object to being treated like a housekeeper. You've told me that you married her because you were attracted to her."

"I am," he said. "She was a vision getting off that stage."

"Are you having second thoughts?"

"No, even now, I can't wait to get in the house and show

her I care about her. I want to make things work with Minnie. Today, I was shocked."

Today, he let the past get between him and Minnie. His father was right that they couldn't bring back his sister. They had no way of knowing who this man was. Yet, his interest was piqued.

With a sigh, he stood from brushing the horse. He needed to turn his attention to his wife. To Minnie.

"Son, your priority has to be your wife," his father told him.

If he could figure out this man, then he could move on with his life.

"Pops, aren't you curious about GBH?"

For a moment, his father paused. "Have you not been listening to me? Shove those damn initials out of your head and concentrate on what's important. Your wife."

Oh, how he wanted to, but didn't his sister deserve justice? Didn't the man who got her pregnant and wasn't at her side when she and the baby died, didn't he deserve an ass whooping at least?

For now, he knew he had to put what he learned this afternoon out of his mind and concentrate on his marriage. That was what was supposed to happen today. But there was no way he could forget about Beth's lover.

"All right, I'll stop thinking about who the bastard is who took advantage of my sister."

"Thank you," his father said. "Now, I think you better go pay some attention to your wife."

Tossing the brush into a bucket, he gave the horse a pat and then fed them oats before he walked out the barn.

When he entered the house, Minnie was not in the living

area. Opening the door to their bedroom, he found her lying in the bed, fast asleep. Staring at his beautiful wife, it was all he could do not to crawl in bed with her and kiss her from head to toe. As he stared at her, he made a vow. He would make Minnie fall in love with him.

Quietly he shut the door and let her sleep. She didn't wake to eat supper but slept through until the next morning.

All Tripp could do was think about how he let Minnie down. How he let Beth down.

CHAPTER 9

Just when she started to believe that maybe this marriage would work, Tripp disappointed her. How did she compete with a dead sister? She had looked forward to seeing the ranch and spending time with Tripp and then it was almost like he disappeared inside himself.

His sentences were clipped and the afternoon was not how she expected it to turn out. What had she done? Had she made another mistake and married a man who was nothing like she dreamed?

This morning he'd been gone when she awakened. His clothes from yesterday were strewn about the room. One thing she quickly learned about her husband was that he was a slob.

Rising from the bed, she quickly dressed and then picked up his clothes. There were times she missed her servants.

It was one thing to deal with one's own clothing, but she'd be damned if she was going to pick up after him. Clothes that were dirty would simply disappear until he asked where they went.

After yesterday, it was the least she could do to him.

When she walked into the main area of the house, Loyd stood. "Good morning. I was starting to get worried about you."

"Sorry, I must still be recovering from the trip. I didn't expect to sleep so long. Where's Tripp?"

"Oh, he's out in the field working. He won't be back until late this evening. He's moving the cattle closer to the house for winter. When there's three feet of snow on the ground, it's hard to feed the animals when they're at the edge of the property."

The thought of snow made her smile. Yes, it would be cold, but she had never seen the white stuff falling from the sky. Only read about it in books.

The baby would need warmer clothes and she would need to get started making them right away.

"Since I lived in the city, I have no idea what is done when you own a ranch."

He grinned. "Neither did my wife, but soon I think she knew more than I did."

Minnie grinned. She liked Tripp's father. For the last two days, he had tried to make her feel at ease and she appreciated that. Adjusting to living with a man was more difficult than she imagined. Especially, when love was not involved.

"Today, I thought I would make a roast. Want to help me?"

"Yes," she said, thinking she'd never cooked a day in her life. They had a live-in cook and a housekeeper. Maybe if she learned to cook, Tripp would appreciate her more as a woman. Maybe if she learned more about ranching, he would accept her into his life.

That's all she wanted. A husband who would love her and the baby. She didn't expect a miracle over night, but she wanted a man who cared.

For the next hour, Loyd and she worked the chunk of beef he had brought up from the root cellar. A colder place, she'd never been, but knew it kept the meat from spoiling.

He showed her how to add potatoes and spices to the meat. When they were finished, he lit the oven and then slid the pan in.

"Now, we'll have supper in about six hours," he said. "In the meantime, why don't we make some cookies. It's been years since we had cookies. Sugar cookies are some of Tripp's favorites."

Cook used to make sugar cookies and they were the best. Oh, how she wished she had watched her. Today, she would try to make a batch of her own.

Loyd helped her mix the ingredients. "Your mother never showed you how to make cookies?"

She laughed. "My mother was a socialite in Charleston. She had servants who cooked and made cookies. She attended teas, balls, and what I called gossip circles. Ladies who sat around and told on their neighbors."

"What kind of life is that?" Loyd asked. "What did she teach you girls?"

"She taught me and my sister, Nora, how to set a table, host dinner parties, needlework, and write the perfect social invitation to people you know. But no housekeeping skills were taught."

Loyd shook his head as he helped her roll out the cookie

dough. The baby gave a big kick as if giving its approval of cookies.

"Oh," she said.

"That baby looks like he's growing more and more each day. In the three days you've been here, I think he's grown."

She glanced down at her waist. "Are you going to be all right with a grandchild that's not Tripp's."

He laughed. "Babies are blessings and that one will be loved and welcomed into this house just as much as the next one you have. Maybe even more because that's what brought you to our home."

Tears swelled up in her eyes. How had she gotten so lucky? "Thank you for being so accepting of me and the baby."

Loyd reached over and wrapped his arm around her shoulder and gave her a sideways hug. "I'm thrilled that my son had the good sense to marry you. Sometimes I wonder what you see in him, but you're going to be very good for him."

She smiled. "He's a good man."

"Yes, he is, but he's a little stubborn."

She laughed as she thought of his reaction yesterday. But if she were a man, would she have responded the same way?

Using a biscuit cutter, he showed her how to cut the shapes and then added a dash of cinnamon and sugar to them before they placed them on the cookie sheet. Moving the roast over, he slid the pan in beside their supper.

"Now we will watch them cook for twelve to fourteen minutes."

"That was fun," she said. She could master cooking if this was all there was to it.

"My wife used to make these for the kids all the time. Not

a day goes by that I don't think about her and miss her by my side. Tell me about your parent's marriage," Loyd said, staring at her.

Her father had always been the more loving and forgiving parent. While her mother worried about whether the neighbors were talking about them.

And then Minnie became pregnant. The night she told her mother, you would have thought the South was once again bombing the city.

"My father died in the Civil War. Papa always read to us a bedtime story in the evenings and then he would kiss us goodnight. He called us *his girls*. Mother, she was more reserved. But when she learned that Papa had been killed, she broke down. I'd never seen her cry before."

It was the one time she realized how much her mother loved her father.

Loyd nodded. "Sometimes people aren't as open with their affection for one another. But it's good for children to see their parents are in love. It's gives them a foundation and then when they marry, they're not afraid to express their emotions. Give Tripp some time. He'll come around."

Her father-in-law believed that Tripp would care about her? Express his emotions and show her affection. She truly hoped so, because a life without love would not work.

She'd jump on the next stage out of town and go home to Charleston before she would live without love.

That evening, supper was on the table when Tripp came in from the fields.

She spent the afternoon cleaning the floors and when he came in with his muddy boots, she met him at the door.

"Boots stay outside," she told him.

He gazed at her like she had lost her mind.

"They'll be cold," he said.

"Maybe you could build a shoe stand for them to sit on inside the door. I'll make a rug to go under it and catch the mud. But I spent all afternoon cleaning this floor. You're not going to mess it up with your muddy boots."

He glanced at his father, who turned his head, a snicker coming from him.

"Pops?"

"You heard her, son. Look how much better the floors look. We've become slobs since your sister died. Remember how she use to fuss when we walked in with muddy boots on."

Tripp reached down and removed his boots and set them by the door. "I'm not leaving them outside."

"That's fine," she said with a smile.

"You're pregnant. Why were you cleaning the floors?"

"Because they were dirty. There were places mud was caked on and Pops had to get a knife and scrape it off. We'll soon have a baby in the house, and we don't want her crawling over a dirty floor."

A frown crossed Tripp's face and yet he didn't argue. She handed him a pair of clean house slippers. The look he gave the shoes almost had her laughing.

"The reason these look so new is because I haven't worn them," he told her.

"Maybe while you're in the house, you should consider them. Wash up. Supper is ready."

She turned and went into the kitchen. The sugar cookies were sitting in a bowl on top of the stove. Thirty minutes ago, she had put on a jar of canned green beans that Pops told her would go well with the roast.

After one day in the kitchen, she was feeling a little more comfortable and knew with Loyd's help, she could tackle the cooking.

Taking the pan out of the oven, she put it on the table that she had carefully set with the dishes and silverware and even a few napkins she found.

No, it wasn't the exquisite table her mother always prepared, but it was homey and would work for her rugged men.

Tripp came into the kitchen and glanced around. His hand immediately reached for a sugar cookie and she slapped it away. "Have you washed up yet?"

"No, that's what I came in here for," he said, grinning at her. Suddenly his hand grabbed hers and he pulled her in tightly against him. "Did you cook the roast?"

A flutter of heat spread through her as her husband's arms held her. A rush of desire spiraled down to her center.

"Your father and I made it together. Then we made the cookies," she said, enjoying the way he smelled of the outdoors. She gazed into his blue eyes and hoped that someday one of their children would have his eyes.

"Give you a little womanly knowledge and you get all kinds of feisty."

She smiled. "It's my first day on the job. Tomorrow, I'm going to tackle our bedroom."

"Oh no," he said. "I'll come back and won't be able to find my long johns. I'll just have to go without."

A blush flooded her cheeks. Though he slept in his long johns, she'd never seen her husband nude. Even now, she could feel his strong muscular chest. For that matter, she'd never seen a man without his clothes and she was curious.

Was her husband flirting with her?

"Mr. Maddox, you'll send me into labor," she said, grinning at him.

"Well, we can't have that can we. At least not yet," he said as he reached down and brushed his lips against her own.

Warmth filled her. Had she at last found a man who would make her happy? Oh, how she hoped.

"Let's eat and if you're a wise man, you'll tell me how wonderful it tastes."

"Mrs. Maddox, anything you cook will make me happy."

When he said her married name, happiness flooded her. It fit and she would make this life fit her.

CHAPTER 10

Two weeks later, Tripp woke Minnie early in the morning. His arms were wrapped around her and his mouth nuzzled her neck. A trickle of heat spread through her and she rolled over to face him.

For the last week when she woke in the morning, he would be kissing the side of her neck or the feel of his arms would be around her. It felt good to wake up beside him and he always brought a smile to her face.

"Good morning," she said.

"What would you think of us going into town today? You need to see the doctor, but I didn't want to rush you since you just arrived. But you and the baby need to be checked out."

She smiled at him. Though they were still adjusting to being married, morning was her favorite time. The feeling of waking in his arms was always a sweet surprise. Sometimes she wished they would linger here in bed with her snuggled up against him, the feel of his rock-hard manhood snug against her bottom.

"Do you feel up to going into town? We could stop at the mercantile and purchase you some warmer clothes. Sooner or later, the snow is going to arrive and stick around all winter long."

"Can I purchase some material to make the baby some warmer clothes? And I would like to mail a letter to my mother and sister."

"Of course," he said, kissing the side of her head.

"Let's go," she said. "Is Pops going with us?"

"No," Tripp said, gazing into her eyes. "We need to spend some time alone. This is our time."

How could she argue with him? He was doing his best to make their marriage work and that made her happy. The thought of spending the day with her husband filled her with joy.

"Do you need to check on the animals this morning?"

"No, Pops will feed them and tonight when we return, I'll take care of them."

Their marriage had taken on a routine of him leaving early in the morning to work with the cattle.

Last week, he moved the herd closer to the house, and in the mornings, she would awaken to the sounds of their moos as they announced the rising of the sun.

It was a pleasant, comforting sound.

"We'll have a quick bite to eat and then get on the road, so we can get home before dark."

The sun was setting earlier and earlier, and she knew he would not want to be traveling in the dark of night.

"Give me a few minutes and I'll be ready."

"Do you need some help getting dressed?" he asked her.

With her belly seeming to grow larger every day, she was having trouble slipping her dresses on and off. Once, she had to ask him for help.

"I think I can manage, but I'll call you if I need help," she said with a shy smile. He had only seen her in her nightgown. They had yet to have sex and had not even discussed it and she knew that sooner or later, they would.

Tripp threw back the covers and a chill swept over her.

"It's cold."

"Wait until the snow falls. Then it gets really cold and we may not go into town for months."

Slowly she sat on the edge of the bed and reached for her wrapper. It took Tripp only a matter of moments to dress and head out the door.

It took her a little longer as she pulled on her heaviest dress. Most of her clothes were lightweight cotton and even her coat was more of a large shawl than protection against the cold.

When she came out ready to go, Tripp and Pops had breakfast ready.

"You kids be careful. Tripp, don't let her get over tired. Sit down and rest."

Pops was always concerned with her well-being and she felt grateful at how he had accepted her.

After they ate, he bundled her up and then helped her into the waiting wagon. After wrapping a heavy lap throw over her, he climbed onto the seat beside her. Releasing the brake, he turned the horses down the road.

She enjoyed watching how he handled the horses. His large hands gripping the reins.

It was the first time she'd truly seen the road from town. That first day had been a blur of nerves and fear and thinking of what she had done.

But today, she saw the pine trees, the rolling hills, and the way the birds flitted from tree to tree chirping at one another. The smell of pine was heavy in the air and she breathed the sweet, clean scent.

Charleston often smelled of the ocean or gunpowder during the war. Or the stench of death. She would never forget the battles that raged while they hunkered down in the lowest part of the house.

"How long has your family lived here?" she asked.

"Pops and mother moved here when Beth and I were babies. They came from Missouri. Even then, the battle over slaves was raging in the state. Pops wanted as far away as possible from the fights between slave owners and those who were against it. In fact, they witnessed a terrible fight that left one man dead and that's when my mother said it was time to go. She didn't want her children raised around killing. So they moved here."

Oh, how she wished she had met his mother, but the woman had been dead for a couple years.

"What about you? How long did your family live in Charleston?"

"My great-grandfather was one of the original colonists. My mother's family were merchants who had ships that traveled the world. They were extremely rich and snooty."

He laughed. Listening to his laughter warmed her insides.

"My sister Nora and I called them the *pretentious pirates*. There were tales of how they had taken from pirates. Who knows if they are true? We didn't like that side of the family much."

He grinned at her. "Minnie, I want you know I'm so glad that I married you. No, we're not completely man and wife yet, but soon. Very soon. I wanted to wait until we were certain we would even like each other."

Even she realized that not many men would have been as patient, but Tripp was making certain they were both ready. She only hoped he didn't wait until she was too big.

A part of her was curious about having sex with her husband, but the thought made her shiver when she remembered her first time.

When they reached the town, he pulled the wagon in front of the doctor's office.

Tripp helped Minnie down. "First, let's see the doctor and then we'll get a bite to eat before we head down to the mercantile."

She placed her hand on his arm and smiled at her husband. Just touching him made her giddy and she liked that feeling.

When they entered the small house, a man came out to meet them.

"Dr. Walker, I'd like you to meet my wife, Minnie Maddox," Tripp said.

"Good to meet you, Mrs. Maddox, and it looks like you have a little one on the way," he said smiling.

Would he refuse to see her? Would he embarrass her in front of Tripp?

"Yes, sir," she said, running her hand over her belly. No matter what, she always felt protective of her child.

"Are you here for a check-up?" the doctor asked.

"Yes," they both said and smiled.

"Well, come on back and let's see how this little one is doing," he said.

With trepidation, she followed him to the examination room. Was here where he would tell her to leave and never come back?

When they walked into the room, the doctor pulled out a tape measure and measured her belly. Next, he listened to her heart and then he placed a horn shaped instrument on her swollen stomach.

"This is a Pinard horn and it lets me hear the baby's heartbeat. Very strong sounding heart," he said. "How far along do you think you are?"

It was a night she would never forget. The only time she'd ever had sex and it had not been a pleasant experience. She often wondered when she had sex with Tripp if it would be as terrible as when she did with Richard.

"March thirtieth was the date of conception," she said.

The doctor frowned. "How can you be so certain?"

What? Did he want the gory details of how Richard had refused to listen to the word no? "That's the date."

The doctor's expression changed and she realized he knew. He understood that it had been a one-time occurrence, not of her choice.

"That would make you due right around Christmas. Now babies come early and some babies are stubborn and come late. So don't hold me to that date."

The baby would come when it was ready to face the world and not a moment before.

"Are you feeling all right?" he asked.

"I'm fine," she said. Besides having to pee all the time and feeling like she would never be thin again. And her emotions rising and falling like a stormy sea.

"Doctor, we live a good hour from town. Should we move into town for a while, closer to the due date?"

The doctor shrugged. "That's up to you, but first babies are slow, and I can reach the ranch before this one arrives."

Tripp tensed and she realized he wasn't happy with the doctor's response, but he didn't say anything.

"Mrs. Maddox, we're about six weeks from Christmas. The next time I see you, you'll be in labor."

Six weeks before this baby arrived – until she saw the little one she already loved so very much.

Tripp frowned. "Doctor, one other question. Is it all right if we have sex?"

What was he doing?

"Of course. As long as Mrs. Maddox is up to it, there shouldn't be any problems."

Her chest tightened. Minnie felt her cheeks flame. She wanted the floor to open up and for her to drop to where no one would see her. Tripp was asking the doctor about sex?

Turning, she walked toward the front office wanting to escape while the men were talking about the complications of having sex with a pregnant woman.

Dear God. Was that the reason Tripp wanted to come to town and for her to see a doctor?

She stepped outside the doctor's office and breathed the fresh air of Angel Creek and watched as the people bustled about the small town.

The door closed behind her and she turned and shook her head. "How could you?"

"What?"

"Ask him about us having sex. I'm so embarrassed."

"Because, honey, I'm your husband and I can't wait to do more than just sleep beside you in bed."

A blush spread across her face. Tripp wanted to have sex with her, even in her enlarged pregnant state.

CHAPTER 11

Tripp had been relieved to see the old doctor was no longer there. The one who announced the death of Beth and the baby. But he worried about them being so far from town. Sure the older doctor had made it out to the ranch in time, but Beth and the baby were already in distress.

And there was nothing he could do to save them. Tripp did not want to lose a wife the same way he'd lost a sister and niece. He almost waited until she was out the door to ask him if he had any reason to worry about this happening again. But didn't because he feared her coming back in.

As they walked down the street, he enjoyed the sights of the frontier town, but he enjoyed the quiet of the ranch more. Glancing over, he realized his wife was upset.

Minnie was not happy that he asked the doctor about having sex, but his wife was beautiful. He was growing more and more attracted to her every day. The longer they slept together, the more he wanted her, and he hoped she wanted him as well.

As a man, he ached to touch his wife. Experience making love to her.

But did pregnant women have desires? It seemed a little awkward and not a question she would have approved of him asking the doctor. In fact, she wasn't happy that he asked about sex. Was it wrong to make certain he could have sex with his wife without harming her or the child?

After all, he was a man and his wife left him hard and wanting, which was a good thing.

He took her by the arm and gazed down at her. "I'm sorry if I embarrassed you, but I wanted to make certain it was all right. I worry about harming you or the baby. If you want to wait until after the baby is born, we will."

She licked her lips. "It's just not a subject I felt comfortable talking about."

How could his wife be so innocent and yet pregnant with another man's child? He'd seen the way she reacted when the doctor asked about the conception time. She knew the exact date.

Had the man taken advantage of her? Soon, he was going to ask her but not until he felt certain she was ready to talk about the father and what happened.

Telling him how she got pregnant had to be her decision and he hoped that someday she would trust him enough to tell what went wrong between the father and her.

If the man had taken advantage of her, he better never show his face in town, or he would be a dead man. "Let's get a bite to eat and then we'll go shopping. Are you feeling all right? You're not too tired, are you?"

No matter what today, he had to be thinking of her welfare.

"I'm fine. Hungry, but I feel good. The sun is shining and we're going to the mercantile to buy me some warmer clothes."

He grinned at her and picked up the back of her hand and kissed it. "Let's go eat, Mrs. Maddox."

A smile graced her lips and it was all he could do not to reach down and kiss her right here on Main Street.

When they entered the cafe, it was filled with working men. Miners, ranchers, and even the banker. Tripp tipped his cowboy hat at some of the men as they made their way inside The Eatery.

"Tripp, Minnie, please join us," Ginger Carroll, the preacher's wife, said. Sitting beside her was her husband, Flint.

The woman stood and gave Minnie a hug. "From one pregnant woman to another. How are you doing?"

"I'm good. Oh my, you've gotten so big."

"Yes, this baby is due just any day now and I told Flint I was not cooking. I'm tired, cranky, and this child is practicing to be a rodeo star the way he's moving around."

Tripp gazed in awe at the two women. After meeting the day of the wedding, he could see they were friends. Ginger didn't ask questions but accepted his wife like she'd known her all her life.

Gratitude filled him.

He reached out and shook Flint's hand. "Good to see you, preacher. Looks like any day now, you're going to be a father."

"You won't be far behind me," he said smiling.

"No, we just came from the doctor's office and he is saying around Christmas."

"Why don't the two of you join us," Flint said.

Tripp glanced at Minnie and she nodded. It was good that she was making friends in town.

They sat at the table. "How's married life treating you?"

Minnie turned and glanced at Tripp a shy smile on her face.

"I think good. How about you, Minnie?" Tripp asked, not wanting to respond for his wife.

"It's been very good. Pops is teaching me to cook and Tripp and I are figuring out how to live together."

It wasn't a resounding endorsement, but it wasn't bad. And most of all, it was true. Tripp didn't know what his expectations of married life were, but so far he liked having a warm body to cuddle with, someone to talk to and a gorgeous woman to gaze at.

"Oh, those first few weeks are the hardest," Ginger said. "I would set the house up one way and he would come behind me and change it. We do things so very different. But..." she grinned at her husband, "we both made adjustments and now I can't imagine a day without him beside me."

Tripp smiled at the couple. Someday he hoped that Minnie would talk about him that way. Someday, he wanted his wife to love him with her heart and soul just like he was beginning to fall for her.

The waitress took their order.

"Is the nursery ready for the new baby?" Minnie asked.

Ginger smiled. "Yes, my sweet husband finished it yesterday. With the baby coming just anytime, we were rushing to get things done. But now we're ready."

"I'm so happy for the two of you," Minnie told her.

"And soon your baby will arrive. We will have to get together and let them play once they're older."

"I would love that," Minnie said.

The two men sat there and shook their heads at their wives. Tripp felt included for the first time in a long time. Sure, he grew up in Angel Creek, but they lived so far out of town, that it was hard to get to know many kids.

That's why he and Beth were so close. The thought that Beth's child would have been fourteen months old had him sighing. There were days he still missed her.

Suddenly Ginger gasped. She grabbed Flint by the arm. "We need to go. My water just broke."

His eyes widened and he stood almost knocking over the table. "Great seeing you, folks, but I think we're going to have a baby. A baby. Dear God, we're going to have a baby. Sweet Jesus, help me."

The man kept saying the words over and over.

"Good luck, Ginger," Minnie called out. "I would have hugged her, but they were in shock."

"Yes, Flint was a bit of a wild, confused man. It will be hours, but I'm sure he wanted to get her home."

They looked at each other and grinned. "Soon that will be us."

"Yes," Tripp said, fear squeezing his chest. Death during delivery couldn't happen a second time. Not like Beth. Not Minnie.

CHAPTER 12

An hour later, they walked out of the restaurant and crossed the street on their way to the mercantile. Minnie could feel herself growing tired but didn't want to spoil their fun.

Plus, she was enjoying spending time with Tripp. Getting to know him.

"We'll stop in the mercantile, purchase the items we need, and I can introduce you to Jeremiah and Cassie," Tripp said.

At the building entrance, Tripp held the door open. She walked over to an aisle that contained bolts of material.

Tripp was beside her. "Let's get you a new coat and also some boots. You're going to need boots in the snow, which should arrive just about any day now."

This felt awkward. She was accustomed to purchasing anything she wanted and putting it on her father's account. But this was her husband and she didn't want to appear greedy. How much could she spend?

"Tripp," a man called, walking up to him and shaking his hand. "Good to see you. And who is this?"

"My wife, Minnie," Tripp said.

A woman came from behind a counter and hurried to Tripp. "I heard you got married. Congratulations, you two."

She glanced at Minnie's belly, but she didn't say a word and for that, Minnie felt grateful.

"You need a coat," the woman said, glancing at her. "Come with me."

She took her by the arm and led her to some coats hanging on a rack. "There's not much of a selection, but it's going to get cold any day now. Normally, this time of year, we already have snow."

"Thank you," Minnie said.

"The whole town is talking about the mail order bride who caught Tripp Maddox. He's always been a looker, but kind of stand offish, if you know what I mean. Of course, there are very few single women here in town."

If the woman thought she was telling Minnie, something she didn't know, she was wrong. Her handsome husband could be withdrawn, but if that was his worst fault, then so be it.

Minnie smiled. "He's a good man and I'm so lucky to have married him."

The woman took the coat off the hook. "Here, let me help you put it on."

She slipped the coat over Minnie's very round belly.

"That baby is going to be arriving soon," she said.

"Yes," Minnie replied not willing to explain to her how Tripp had taken her in.

"Do you have any long johns?"

"No," Minnie said, thinking how in the world could she get them up and over her ever-expanding belly.

"You're going to need some. We normally sell out the first cold spell of the season, so don't wait until after the baby comes to get some. Also you're going to need boots."

She led her to a bench and helped her sit. Then she brought her different styles of boots.

Minnie felt odd not doing this with Tripp. After all, it was his money that would be purchasing these items and she didn't want to get too much. But she had to have some material. The baby didn't have any clothes except for a few things her mother insisted she take with her from Charleston. Little outfits that would never keep the baby warm.

"Try this boot on," Cassie said. "Too snug?"

"Yes," Minnie said, looking around for Tripp.

Just then the door opened to the mercantile and Cassie stood. "Oh no. I'll be right back," she said as she hurried behind the counter.

What was going on?

"Robert, what do you need?"

Oh no, Minnie thought as she slowly stood. Robert Larsen was approaching her husband. Fear spiraled through Minnie and she clutched her stomach.

"Nothing," he said, not looking at Cassie. "Tripp, how do you like having two men's leftovers. The man who got her pregnant and mine."

Minnie watched in horror as her husband's face turned red and then he doubled his fist and punched Robert.

The man fell and Tripp stood over him. "I'm not the one who walked away from a woman in need. Don't you ever mention my wife again, do you understand me? Next time, I won't punch you, I'll kill you. Now get the hell out of the store."

Tripp didn't wait for the man to stand, but rather grabbed his shirt and dragged him out the door.

"Stop," he called. "I'm going to the sheriff."

"Please do, so I can tell him how you treat women," Tripp said.

Jeremiah held the door open and Tripp tossed him out into the street. Minnie ran in her stocking feet to her husband.

She grabbed his hand and stared into his sky-blue eyes that radiated hate. "Are you all right? You didn't get hurt, did you?"

Taking his hand in hers, she rubbed it, soothing the cuts. Tripp had risked his life standing up for her. No man had ever done that and her heart swelled. Tripp defended her honor.

For a moment, they stood there staring at one another and she felt like the earth moved beneath her feet. No other man had protected her like Tripp, and she felt her heart pounding in her chest.

"You gonna be able to drive a wagon home?" Jeremiah asked, bringing them both back to where they were.

"I'm fine. Really," Tripp said. "I'm sorry, but he had that coming."

Cassie smiled at him. "Of course, he did. He disrespected your lovely wife."

"Are you almost done?" Tripp said. "We should probably be heading for home. The clouds are starting to build, and I don't want to get caught in a storm."

Minnie reached up and ran her hand down his cheek. "Thank you. You didn't have to hit him."

"Oh yes, I did," Tripp said and she could see he was still

furious. "You're my wife and I'm your protector. No one gets away with hurting you."

Emotions flowed through her at the words her husband said.

"Thank you," she said and hugged him, though her belly was beginning to make that impossible.

Jeremiah and Cassie smiled at one another.

"Come on, let's get you some boots," she said, taking Minnie by the hand.

Minnie let go of Tripp and went with Cassie, but her heart wanted to remain to make certain her husband was all right.

"That Robert is a troublesome man. You should be thankful you didn't marry him."

Every day she thanked God that he had rejected her and Tripp had asked her to marry him.

Minnie nodded as she tried on a pair of boots and really liked the way they made her feet feel. "I need to get three yards of material to make some baby blankets and little outfits."

"Of course," Cassie said. "You're so lucky to have married Tripp. He's a great man."

That was how Minnie felt as well. Today, he'd defended her from Robert Larsen. Thank goodness, she hadn't married such a snake.

The thought of how close she'd come to saying *I do* with that evil man sent a shiver through her.

"Come on," Cassie said. "I'll pack up your stuff and even throw in a pair of baby booties. That little one will need something to keep his feet warm."

"Thank you," Minnie said and then gazed at her husband who was in a deep conversation with Jeremiah.

Were they talking about Robert or was he still searching for the man whose initials were beside Beth's?

CHAPTER 13

Jeremiah had to calm Tripp down after the confrontation with Robert. The urge to beat the man into a bloody pulp almost overcame him, but the thought of Minnie seeing him at his worst calmed Tripp.

No, he wasn't one for losing his temper, but no man had the right to treat a woman that way. No one. But then he also felt ecstatic that he had refused to marry Minnie.

Because then she became Tripp's wife and he would defend her with his last breath. Even during the short time they were married, he knew she was his woman and no one else's.

No one said anything bad about his woman unless they wanted to meet his fists.

Outside the store, he helped her into the wagon. The clouds were gathering. A storm was brewing and they needed to get home.

Taking the lap robe, he tucked her inside. "It's going to

storm. Let's hope we make it home before the weather turns nasty."

Her emerald eyes grew large. "Is it going to snow?"

Walking around the wagon, he climbed up and watched his wife acting like she was ten not nearly twenty. The woman got excited about the strangest things. But then again, he had grown up with blizzards and the wild weather snow could bring.

"Maybe," he said, grinning at her as she bounced up and down on the seat in the wagon.

"I've never seen snow. Can we build a snowman when we get home?"

He glanced at his very pregnant wife like she was crazy. "No, it will be getting dark and I'm not going to let you slip and fall."

She pouted and he'd never seen that before. With her full lips pursed, it was all he could do not to give her a kiss that would chase the chill away. Laughing, he reached over and kissed lightly her on the lips. "Keep that up and I'll kiss you the way I want to in front of the whole town."

Yes, the woman was big with child, but she was beautiful, and someday he would make her belly swell with his baby.

"You wouldn't," she said, her eyes growing large.

"Try me."

Grabbing the reins, he released the brake and clicked to the horses, who started up the street.

"Is your hand all right?"

"It's going to be sore," he said, thinking it hurt like hell, but he had to drive them home.

"Cassie told me Robert was a bad man and that I should consider myself lucky I didn't marry him."

The thought of that man mistreating his wife and child was enough to cause Tripp's anger to rise again. No, the baby wasn't his, but the moment he married Minnie, he took on the responsibility of that child.

Now he considered that baby his.

"I know," he said.

"Thank you for introducing me to Jeremiah and Cassie. She helped me with the coat and the boots. I didn't spend too much money, did I? If I did, I have a little I can give you."

He turned and gazed at her. "You are my wife and I'll provide for you and our baby. No, you didn't spend too much. Keep your money."

She smiled at him. "Why are you so good to me?"

He grinned at her. "Because I want to be. Because you deserve a man who takes care of you."

Because he was the luckiest man in Montana to have married Minnie before all the single men found out she was available.

The clouds grew darker, but he was afraid to make the horses go faster. In Minnie's condition, she couldn't take bouncing around on the seat of the wagon.

"Thank you," she whispered, and he could see tears welling up in her eyes.

"So you've forgiven me for asking the doctor if we could have sex?"

Shaking her head, she laughed. "Of course. Just promise me you will take it easy with me. I've only had sex once and it wasn't fun."

A frown crossed his face. What did she mean it wasn't fun? "Did he force himself on you?"

"I believed he was going to marry him. We talked about when we would announce our engagement. One night taking me home from meeting his parents, right there in the carriage, he crawled on top of me and when I told him no, he told me to shut up."

Rage consumed Tripp and he wanted to go to Charleston and pummel this bastard.

"He refused to stop."

Tripp glanced at his wife and her face was white. Even in the cold, he could see how the memory affected her.

What a low life bastard. If that was what happened to his sister, he would kill the man when he found him.

"What did he do when you told him about the baby?"

She laughed, the sound empty and hollow. "Suddenly he disappeared. Whenever I sent him a message, he never responded. When I went to his home, he was never there. It was like he just vanished. Then I read in the paper that he was getting married."

This man was the worst. If he ever met him, he wouldn't live to see the next day.

"Again, he refused to see me or talk to me. So I went to the wedding. A very exclusive event that only the most prestigious society people in Charleston were invited to."

Tripp started laughing. Knowing Minnie, he could only imagine what she'd done.

"When it came to that part about if anyone objects to this marriage, I stood and said *I do. I'm expecting his child.*"

Already he could just picture the scene of his lovely wife standing and announcing her pregnancy to the crowd of high society snobs.

"What happened?"

He gave her a quick glance before returning his eyes to the road.

"His bride fainted. His servants came and walked me out the door. Her family halted the happy event. Eventually, her father came to see me and we talked. Last I heard, the wedding was permanently off."

"Did he ever talk to you about the child?"

"Never. In fact, I heard that his family sent him to Texas for a while. My own mother told me I needed to get out of town. That I had branded myself and my child with scandal. Not to mention my little sister."

A boom of thunder echoed in the mountains. They were getting close to home, but still had at least thirty minutes to go. He drove around a huge hole in the road, the wagon bouncing.

The skies were darkening. Any moment, he expected snowflakes to start flying.

"Mother found Robert's ad in the Mail Order Bride Gazette and here I am."

Tripp reached over with his sore hand and patted her on the leg. Then he ran his hand up to her belly. "And because of his stupidity, I have the most beautiful wife in town and a baby coming."

"You don't regret marrying me?"

A quick glance confirmed she worried he had changed his mind. What she didn't realize was how much he wanted to consummate their marriage. But now after hearing her story, he was glad they waited.

"Never. I'm glad you're here. You had a horrible experience. I promise you that when we have sex, it won't be like that. And I'm not leaving you. We're married and this baby is mine."

She picked up his hand and raised it to her lips and kissed the inside of his palm. A shiver of desire traveled up his spine. How much more could he take?

He felt like he was the luckiest man alive and yet the fear of what had happened to Beth rode him hard each day. He couldn't lose Minnie like he had Beth. He just couldn't.

"What are you going to tell the baby?"

"Nothing," she said. "Not until she or he's old enough to realize that something isn't right about their birthday. Then I'll tell them the truth."

He nodded. That was smart. Just then the first snowflakes of the season began to drift down like fluffs of sugar landing on their clothing.

"It's snowing," she cried, excitement causing her emerald eyes to grow large.

He glanced at his wife sticking her tongue out trying to catch the flakes. A grin spread across his face. This woman was part child and all woman and he could feel love for her growing.

"Are you warm enough?"

"Yes," she said. "My first snowflakes."

A laugh came from his chest. "By April, you'll be sick of them."

"By April, the baby will be four months old." She gazed at him, her eyes shining with tears. "I'm going to be a mother. What if I can't do this?"

Stunned, he stared as his wife had an emotional outburst and he realized she was afraid. After everything she'd been through, he had no doubts about the kind of mother she would be.

"Are you joking? A woman who traveled halfway across the country to give her child a better life? You're going to be a great mother. And I'll be right there at your side."

CHAPTER 14

$\mathcal{B}$y the time the wagon pulled up in front of the house, the ground was beginning to look white.

"Pops, it's snowing," Minnie said excitedly when the man came out to greet them.

"I was getting worried. Looks like this could be quite a storm. Mrs. Minnie, you sit tight. We don't need you slipping and falling."

Her new family really did take care of her. Tripp came around and lifted her out of the wagon. For a second, he held her close and she loved the way he smelled of leather.

"Get in the house and stay there."

"I thought we could build a snowman," she said.

"Not tonight. There isn't enough snow," he said, shaking his head at her, his blue eyes dancing with laughter as the snow from his hat fell on her.

"Hey, you're getting me wet," she said as happiness filled her. Today, she'd told Tripp about how she'd gotten pregnant and he promised her sex would be different. He had not condemned her, but rather seemed angry that this happened to her.

No one had listened to her, not even her mother. But Tripp did and that filled her with joy. It was awful to be blamed for something you had no control over.

Though she would be nervous, she knew she had to trust Tripp. He was a man of his word and she felt certain he would take care of her.

"Good, now go inside with Pops. I'll be there as soon as I put the horses up."

He lifted her items from the back of the wagon and handed them to her.

The baby material. Anticipation had her fingering the material inside the cloth bag Cassie gave her.

"Look, Pops, I'm going to make the baby some clothes," she said, running her hand over the material as she walked up on the porch under the awning.

"You know there might be some baby items in a chest somewhere. Let me see if I can find them tomorrow. Right now, let's get you in the house out of the cold. Did you have a good doctor's appointment?"

"Yes," she said. "He said the baby will arrive sometime around Christmas."

"A Christmas baby."

"Yes," she said, feeling excitement that soon she would be holding the infant.

"Did you and Tripp have a good time?"

"Yes, Pops. Though we were having lunch with Flint and Ginger Carroll, the preacher and his wife, when she went into labor."

It was the first time she'd ever been around someone in labor and she wondered how Ginger was doing. Had the baby arrived yet?

"That's exciting. You know I think we need to get a nursery prepared. We only have about six weeks before that baby is due to arrive."

She grinned, a feeling of warmth coming over her. She'd been so blessed when she married into this family.

"Thank you, Pops, for accepting this child."

"Of course, it's my grandchild. I can hardly wait," he said as he held open the door.

As they entered the house, she realized that Christmas was only weeks away.

"What do you do for Christmas here on the ranch?"

Pops eyes grew misty. "When my wife was alive, we would cut a tree, put it in the main room and she would decorate it with popcorn and streamers. She even made tiny bows one time to put on the tree."

"Let's do that this year," Minnie said growing excited.

"You're going to be very pregnant and probably won't feel like doing much," he said to her.

This was her first Christmas with Pops and Tripp, and she wanted it to be special. "It's our first Christmas as a family. Next year we'll have a toddler running around. Let's put up a tree this year."

Yes, she would be big, but that didn't mean she wasn't excited about celebrating the holiest time of the year.

The old man shook his head. "We'll talk to Tripp."

Just then the baby decided to do a tap dance in her belly. She smiled as she watched her stomach move.

"You need to rest. I have supper almost ready. Just need to throw in some biscuits."

"I'll set the table," she said, moving about the room to get the dishes.

Pops stood back and watched her, shaking his head. She glanced at him. "What's wrong?"

"Oh how I wish my Emily was here to see you. She would have been so excited about this child. Even Beth."

Beth meant a lot to these men and they had never told her what happened. She wanted to know the story of Tripp's sister. "What happened to Beth?"

Just then a door slammed as Tripp came in. Pops moved to the oven, ignoring her question. She glanced up as Tripp came in.

"It's really coming down out there," he said. "We got home just in time. By morning, we should have several inches."

Giddiness filled her and then she remembered Tripp's hand. "Pops, what can I put on Tripp's hand?"

"It's nothing," he said to her.

Pops moved from the oven and glanced at Tripp's swollen, bruised hand. "What happened?"

Tripp gave her a glance that said do not say anything. "I escorted a man out of the mercantile."

"With your fists?"

"Kind of," he replied.

His father shook his head. "You don't get into fights very often, so I'm thinking you must have run into Robert Larsen."

It was odd that Pops knew immediately who his son tangled with. But then again, it seemed that Robert had quite the reputation.

"The one and only. If he's smart, he won't say anything else."

"The man is not smart," Pops replied, putting the biscuits into the oven. "We'll eat in about twenty minutes."

Pops walked out the front door with a pan in his hand. When he returned, it was filled with snow. "Put your hand in this. It will at least take the swelling down. It's a wonder you didn't break it."

"The man said some unflattering things about Minnie," he told his father.

"Well, it's a good thing then that I wasn't there. We'd both probably be in jail," he said.

Minnie led her husband to the table and had him sit. Then she placed the pan on the table. "Here you go."

She kissed him on the forehead. "Hopefully, there won't be a next time."

The wind rattled the windowpanes. And when she glanced outside all she could see was white. Minnie had never seen anything like it. Not even the occasional hurricane looked like this.

"Oh, yes, winter has arrived," Pops said. "I always know when the windows start rattling, it's going to be a cold one."

"And tomorrow we're going to play in the snow?"

Both men turned and laughed at her. "Tomorrow, it's going to be frigid cold."

Pops shook his head. "And she wants to decorate for Christmas."

The two men glanced at each other and Minnie knew they had not decorated since his wife died.

"She would want us to celebrate the birth of the savior," Minnie said.

Minnie turned and noticed the way Tripp was staring at her. If he kept looking at her that way, he was likely to start a fire. Suddenly the idea of having sex with her husband didn't sound like a bad idea. Especially on a snowy cold night.

CHAPTER 15

*L*ater that night, Tripp came into their bedroom. The wind outside howled and the temperature dipped below freezing. A chill filled the room and he glanced at Minnie snug in the bed reading out loud.

"What are you doing?"

"I'm reading a story to the baby from the Bible. It's the story of Christmas. The night the Savior was born." The same night their baby was due, though it might come early or later. Whenever this child arrived, he just hoped the birth was safe for the mother and child.

Quickly, he shed his pants leaving on his long johns and crawled into bed with his wife.

He lay his head on her lap and she smiled down at him but continued reading.

When she came to the part about the three wise men coming to visit the child, he felt a soft thump.

Stunned, he turned and gazed at her stomach.

"The baby kicked me," he said.

"You felt that?"

"Yes," he said, running his hand over her stomach. He leaned in and kissed her belly.

His wife gasped. "That feels good."

His hands ran over her stretched skin that encircled the growing child.

This woman made him happy in ways he'd never expected and part of him was terrified of losing her.

Pushing that thought from his mind, he rose and kissed her. His lips covered hers as he drank from her. He didn't believe in love at first sight, but yet he'd been drawn to her. Something inside told him she was his. Even though she was now eight months pregnant, he wanted her.

She kissed him back and even dropped her Bible and wrapped her arms around him. "Tripp?"

"Yes, honey," he asked, their lips breaking apart, even though he didn't want to stop kissing her. His lips trailed down her neck, to her shoulder, her chest.

She gasped. "Tripp, I'm fat. I'm big. I'm eight months pregnant."

"You're beautiful," he said. "Each day you grow more beautiful."

"You promise me sex will be different?"

Shock filled Tripp and yet he didn't stop his lips from caressing her. This was what he'd wanted for so long.

"I'll make certain you enjoy having sex and if you're not, tell me and I'll stop. All you have to do is say, *Tripp stop* and I will. I give you my word."

For a moment, she tensed in his arms and then slowly he felt her relax. "Your kisses make me feel things I've never felt."

"I'm glad," he said, smiling while he continued kissing his way down to her breasts.

They were large and full and exquisite.

"All right," she said with a sigh. "Show me how sex will be different with you."

"Yes," he said as he pulled her nightgown up and over her head. "Anytime you want to stop, just tell me."

Oh, how he hoped not to hear that one word tonight. He'd waited so long for this day and he would make it special for her. He promised.

CHAPTER 16

Tripp couldn't stop smiling. Early the next morning, he left his sleeping wife in the bed as he went into the kitchen. Last night the storm outside had dumped a good foot of snow.

The storm in the bedroom had brought them together. Not once had Minnie asked him to stop, and afterward, she'd lain in his arms crying. Not because he'd harmed her in any way, but because she loved the magic they created together.

Because she never dreamed sex could be so beautiful between a man and a woman when it wasn't forced. Hopefully he had banished her bad memories and replaced them with the two of them sharing the most beautiful moment.

Now he felt like they were truly man and wife. That by their joining, her past was erased and she was his and only his. And their baby would soon arrive.

"You're all happy this morning," his father said as he handed him a cup of coffee. "Where's Minnie?"

"She's still sleeping."

His father stopped and jerked back.

"Oh my God, I recognize that look. Years ago, I would have that silly shit-eating grin on my face after your mother and I had a pleasure filled night."

Oh no, he didn't need his father saying anything to Minnie or he would be in trouble.

"Pops, please don't say anything. She'd be mortified."

"Son, I would never do that. You look happy."

"I am, Pops. I truly am."

Both men were silent for a moment. A sense of peace had settled over Tripp, except for his fear of the birth. And he prayed every single day that it would go easily for Minnie.

"The only thing I worry about is her suffering like Beth did."

His father nodded. "Understand. But you're a rancher. How many births do you see that go just fine and then suddenly we have a stubborn calf or a horse that's turned wrong? No sense worrying about what you can't fix until it happens."

That was true, but still the fear lingered, growing like an embankment of snow that suddenly let loose, tumbling down the mountain, killing everything in its path.

"Christmas is coming. She wants to decorate and I think we should. Next year, there will be a little one running around. It's time we brought back the joy of Christmas."

It was true. Since his mother had died, they'd not cared. Even Beth had not wanted to celebrate. But now it was time to put their grief behind them.

"You're right. Mother would want us to continue our traditions and celebrate the holidays."

"Have you thought about what you're going to get Minnie?"

"Not really. Why?"

Pops smiled. "I have an idea and if you don't like it, then just say so. Have you purchased her a wedding ring?"

"No," Tripp said. Not certain where this was going, his heart started to pound in his chest.

"What about your mother's wedding ring? Someday your children are going to inherit it, but what if in the meantime, you gave it to Minnie to wear."

Tripp knew his father still missed his mother every day and that he often would hear him talking to her. So to part with her wedding ring said a lot. His mother wore it every day.

"Are you sure, Pops? I don't want you to feel like you have to give it to her."

His father was looking older and Tripp knew that Pops and Minnie had formed a special bond.

"Yes, I'm certain. You know I wanted you to get married and when you first brought her home, I wasn't certain. But now I realize you choose a wonderful woman. Your mother would have loved her. So, yes, give her the ring."

Warmth spread through Tripp and brought tears to his eyes. Even his father had recognized that he'd chosen an exceptional woman.

"Thanks," Tripp said, knowing it had to be a difficult decision for his father.

Suddenly the bedroom door opened and his wife appeared. Her cheeks were rosy this morning and she smiled at him that secretive smile that made his heart pound harder in his chest.

Today was going to be a great day and he hoped they shared many more nights like last night.

"Good morning," she said.

"Good morning," he said, rising from his chair and going to her. He kissed her on the cheek.

"How are you?"

"I'm good. Ready to play in the snow."

He laughed. "Let's wait at least until this afternoon. Maybe by then the sun will be out and it'll be a little warmer."

Pops glanced between the two of them and Tripp saw him nod. From his expression, he knew his father was happy for him and thinking about his mother.

"Besides, I'm going to teach you how to make stew today. And cornbread."

Though his wife was still learning, he knew she would be a fine cook. Glancing around the room, he remembered his mother standing at the stove. She smiled at him and he had to clear his throat to keep the tears at bay.

If only she were here. She would love Minnie.

Minnie smiled. "You men are already drinking coffee. Can I fix you some eggs?"

"Biscuits are already in the oven. In fact, they should be done now."

"I'll take a fried egg," Tripp said.

"Me too," Pops replied.

"All right, be patient with me, but I'm going to fry us up some eggs."

Tripp watched his wife put on an apron and pull out a pan. In the month she'd been here, already he could see such a change in her demeanor. She was happy.

And he was the happiest one of all. On Christmas, he

would give her his mother's wedding ring and tell her how much he loved her. It seemed like the perfect time.

And his father was right. Not every birth ended in tragedy. Minnie's experience would be completely different, he prayed.

CHAPTER 17

*L*ater that morning, Minnie waited for the sun to come out. The clouds were parting and she could see nearly six inches of snow on the ground.

Enough for a snowman.

Tripp had promised to take her out after it warmed up a bit. But how long would that take? Until next spring?

Excited, she went about her chores, and Pops helped her make a stew and some cornbread. Pops helped her prepare it and they left it cooking slowly on the stove.

After she cleaned off the table from the breakfast dishes, she got out the material she bought. First, she made a pattern. Once she had it the way she wanted, she cut out several diaper shirts. The leftover material would make some baby sacks and blankets.

After she had everything cut out, she sat with needle and thread and began to sew them.

The baby kicked her and her heart blossomed with love. No matter the child's father, she loved this tiny one and couldn't wait to see it face to face.

Tripp came in from the barn and they had a quick bite of lunch and she cleaned up the dishes. Afterward, she returned to the rocker where she sat sewing the baby clothes.

"It's warmed up outside. You still want to build a snowman?"

"Yes," she said, jumping up from the seat.

She threw on her coat, put on her new boots, and Tripp gave her a pair of gloves. When she walked outside, she was stunned at how cold the wind felt blowing against her cheeks.

Never had she been out in such a frigid wind.

"We're not going to stay out here long," he said.

"Show me what to do," she said excitedly.

"You take a small ball of snow and press it in your hands. Then roll it in the snow adding more and more, packing it together."

She bent over and picked up and made a ball of snow. Then she did like he said, but her belly was in the way of her bending over too far. And she feared falling on her head.

"Let me help you," Tripp said. "That baby is in the way."

Together, they rolled the ball. When it was bigger than her belly, she leaned back and gazed at him. "What now?"

"Now, we do it again," he said.

Together they made two more balls. Then Tripp lifted them on top of one another.

She jumped up and down excitedly. "My first snowman. What's next?"

Pops came out of the house. "Here is my donation. Two pieces of charcoal for the eyes and a carrot for the nose." There were carrots in the root cellar from the summer garden. Next year, she would learn to grow a garden and how to can.

There was so much she wanted to learn.

Tripp went into the barn and came back with two sticks he cut off a tree. "Here's his arms."

They put the finishing touches on the snowman and then stood back and admired what they'd done.

"In Charleston, we don't get snow like this."

She saw Tripp bend down, grab some snow, and throw it at her. She gasped.

"Your first snowball fight."

She reached down and soon they were both hurling snowballs at one another. She turned to run, not thinking about how slowly she moved and her boot slid on the slick ground.

With horror, she felt herself falling.

Oh no.

Even though it happened so fast, she maneuvered herself, to land on her back, to protect the baby.

In a second, Tripp was at her side.

"Are you all right?"

She lay there assessing her body. Her back ached from the fall, but the snow seemed to have cushioned her. Breathing hard, she waited for the baby to kick her. Nothing.

"I think so," she said. "Help me up."

"No, lay here for a few more minutes. Let's make certain you're all right."

She didn't want to lay in the wet snow. Already she could feel herself growing cold. "Please, Tripp, help me up. I'm getting wet and cold."

Gently, he helped her to her feet, holding onto her to make certain she didn't fall again.

"You're sure you're all right?"

"No, I'm scared. I want to go in the house."

"Come on," he said.

They had been having so much fun and she could see the fear in his eyes. She could feel her heart beating out of her chest and yet the baby didn't move.

"I'll go fetch the doctor," he said.

"No, stay with me. I think the baby is fine. I don't want you to leave."

Tripp helped her into the house and Pops met them at the door. "You all right?"

"She fell," Tripp said.

"Put her in bed," Pops said, an anxious look on his face. "You need to rest until we know you and the baby are all right."

There was no way that Minnie was going to argue with either of them. She was worried. And since this was her first pregnancy, she had no way of knowing if she had done the child any harm.

Tripp helped her into the bed.

"Sit with me," she said. "I'm scared."

"Me too," he whispered as he kissed her forehead. "I knew better than to let you go outside and play in the snow."

She put her finger to his lips. "It's not your fault. You did what I asked you to do. Sometimes I forget I'm a bulky person now and can't do everything I use to."

"Is the baby moving?" Tripp asked.

"No, but sometimes she sleeps. We're going to pray she's just sleeping."

He laughed. "How do you know it's not a boy."

"I don't. But I'm praying for a girl. Someone who looks like me."

Tripp smiled at her, crawled into the bed and held her. "Then I'm going to hope it's a girl as well."

They lay in each other's arms. "Have you thought about a name?"

The name had not come to her yet. She didn't know why, but she feared she would harm the child if she picked out names. Silly, but it was her little qualm.

"No, I'm trying not to think too much about it yet."

"If it's a girl, would you name it after your mother?"

"No," she said. "Mother was very embarrassed that I was pregnant. She refused to hear me when I told her this was not my fault. She didn't think that Richard would ever do something so vile as force himself on me."

"That must have hurt."

"It did. But my sister was always her favorite."

Tripp squeezed her hand.

"Will we have favorites?" she asked.

"No, at least, I hope not. All of our children will have their own personalities. We may love each one of them a little different, but they will all be treated the same."

She sighed against his chest. "After this baby, give me a little time, but I can't wait to have our child. A boy who looks like you."

As her eyes drifted close, Tripp squeezed her. "I can't wait either."

CHAPTER 18

Minnie stayed in bed the rest of that day, resting. The next morning, the baby woke her with a swift kick to her bladder.

"She moved," she gasped.

Tripp who had not left her side, sat up in bed. "You felt the baby?"

"Yes," she exclaimed laughing. With a sigh, she gave her husband a smile. Together they held onto each other.

Relief crossed his face. "Thank God."

She grinned. "I think I need to get up and move around."

"Are you sure?"

"Absolutely. Come on, there is so much still to prepare."

When they walked into the kitchen, Pops was already there.

"Are you feeling all right?"

"The baby moved. I'm fine," she said smiling. "Let me cook you breakfast."

"No, not today. You need to rest and stay off your feet. I'll do the cooking today," he said.

If the man had his way, she would be back in bed, but she was tired of just lying around.

"Are you certain it's okay for me to check on the cattle?" Tripp asked her, his blue eyes filled with concern.

All night he had stayed right by her side.

A smile flitted across her face and she reached up and caressed his cheek. "Yes, go, I have things to do."

"Pops, keep an eye on her and don't let her do too much."

"Don't worry, son, she's not going anywhere. She's not cooking today or cleaning either. The rocker is the best place for her."

What did they think she was going to do? Run a race? Yesterday, she learned her lesson and planned on spending the day sewing baby clothes.

By mid-afternoon, she was nearly finished with the little shirts and the baby sack she was making, when Pops came in the door, carrying a cradle.

It was of beautiful wooden oak with rocker arms. She gasped with delight. The perfect size for a newborn.

"Thought this might come in handy, so I went out to the barn and retrieved it. It will do for a month or two anyway."

Tears filled her eyes. "It's perfect. She'll fit in there and I can reach over from the bed and rock her."

Was this Beth's or Tripp's cradle? How fortunate that someone had saved it and now her baby would get to use it.

He grinned. "Let me find the mattress."

Pops opened a closed bedroom door. Minnie knew that was Beth's room and she'd never been in there. He came back carrying a pad that fit the cradle perfectly. He also brought some diaper shirts, a sleeping bag, and booties.

"Those are so cute," she said, taking them from him.

Tears welled up in his eyes. "They belonged to my daughter. But she's never going to use them."

Minnie reached out and touched Pops on the arm. "Thank you. It means a lot to me that you gave them to my baby."

She didn't know what happened to Beth, but she had made baby clothes and she had a cradle. Could she have been pregnant? But what happened to her and the baby?

And why were they so silent about her fate?

"When the baby gets older, we'll clean out one of the rooms and get it ready for him or her. Until then, I thought they could sleep in the cradle."

There were two more rooms in the house and yet both bedroom doors were kept closed. She'd never been in those rooms and she was not one to be nosy and peek inside.

"Come now," she said, seeing the sadness on Pop's face. "Put the cradle in the bedroom and I'll wash and clean the mattress. Plus, this afternoon, I'll make blankets. It's hard to believe the baby will be here soon."

He grinned and took the cradle into the bedroom. When he returned, she smiled. "Help me make supper tonight. I'm at a loss as to what to fix."

The man shook his head. "You can help me, but I don't think you need to be on your feet for too long."

"I understand, but I can't lie in that bed all day," she said.

Together, the two of them prepared the evening meal. In the short time she'd been here, she really liked Tripp's father. He reminded her of her own, who she missed dearly. If her father had been alive, Richard would have been forced to marry her. Her papa would have believed her.

But then, she would not have met Tripp. She wondered if the letters she'd sent her mother and sister had arrived yet.

That afternoon she spent sewing clothes and preparing the cradle. The thought that soon a baby would be lying there filled her with joy.

There didn't seem to be any lingering effects from her falling in the snow and she was so thankful. Once again, the baby inside her was active and she knew her snow days were over for a while.

That evening when Tripp came home, she looked up from finishing yet another diaper shirt.

His cheeks and nose were red from the cold when he came in brushing snow from his jacket.

"It's snowing again," he told her.

"I see that," she said. "But I think I will stay inside. You look cold."

"It's freezing," he said. "Are you doing all right?"

"I'm doing great. The baby has been active today, so I feel so much better. But until this child arrives, I've decided you're right. I need to take it easy."

Yesterday had frightened her and she knew the chances of a premature baby surviving were slim. She wanted this child to stay right where it was until the necessary time of its arrival.

"Were the cattle all right?"

"Glad to see me bring hay. Broke the ice on the tanks and they should have enough water now to last them until it freezes tonight."

He sank down beside her on the horsehair couch and picked up a tiny diaper shirt. "Hard to believe that either one of us wore something this small."

"This is what I've been doing all day," she said. "Oh, and I helped your father make supper. It's ready."

"Great, I'm starving," he said, giving her a quick kiss on the cheek. "I'm saving the good stuff until later tonight."

She grinned at him. Having sex with Tripp was a completely different experience. Just thinking about the time they shared in bed had her blushing as she gazed at her husband, knowing she was falling in love with this handsome man.

How had she gotten so lucky?

Tripp stood and she watched him disappear into the room.

Suddenly he cursed. "Minnie."

From his tone, it sounded like he was upset. Awkwardly she rose from the couch and hurried into their bedroom.

"What's wrong," she asked.

He stood gazing down at the cradle, his face an ugly grimace, his eyes flashing with anger.

"Where did you get this cradle?"

"Your father gave it to me. Why? Is something wrong?"

For the first time in their marriage, he turned on her, his fists clenched, his eyes flashing with pain and his face contorted. "He had no right. I'm the one who made this cradle."

She didn't understand why he was so upset.

"If you don't want me using it, then I'll give it back. We'll find something else. But I need to understand why you're so angry. What did I do that was wrong?"

With that, her husband sank down on the bed and put his face in his hands. "I'm sorry. It's not your fault."

"Why are you upset?"

She needed to know because she'd never seen Tripp act this way. Not her easy-going husband. The only other time had been when he became angry when Robert spoke rudely about her.

One thing about the man she was quickly discovering was that if he cared about you, he protected you.

"I made that cradle for Beth's baby," he said. "Just seeing it brought back all the memories of how excited she'd been and then…"

There it was again, the mourning, the sadness regarding Beth. She'd been pregnant, but what happened to her. Slowly it was starting to come together, but she needed confirmation.

"Someone needs to tell me what happened to Beth. You and Pops have been so reticent to say anything about her. Obviously something happened to her, and now I realize, her baby."

Tripp ran his hand down his face and gazed at her, his eyes tearing up.

"She died in childbirth. Her and the baby."

A chill ran through Minnie as she stared at her husband. She went to his side and sat on the bed.

"I'm so sorry. I know you loved her."

Tripp took her in his arms. "In so many ways her story is like yours. No husband. We don't even know who the father is. But he left her and for that I'll never forgive him."

Now she understood so much about her husband. "Did you marry me because I reminded you of Beth?"

He turned and gazed at her. "No, honey, from the moment you stepped off that stage, I was enthralled. I couldn't keep my eyes off you and then when Robert refused to marry you, I knew you were mine."

She hugged him to her as close as she could get with the baby in the way.

"We don't have to use the cradle," she said. "I'll find something else."

"No, it was just a shock when I saw it there. I'm sorry I acted that way. But I'd be honored if our daughter slept in the cradle that I made for Beth's baby."

Hope filled Minnie as she held onto the man who was rapidly claiming her heart. The man she dreamed of spending the rest of her life with. And then the realization slammed into her.

"Are you afraid of me dying?"

For a moment, he was silent and then in an agonized voice, he whispered, "Yes. I'm terrified."

CHAPTER 19

Two weeks later, Tripp saw a man riding in the distance toward the ranch. His coat was pulled tightly against him and he wore his hat low.

He hurried from the barn to the house wanting to be there when whoever this was arrived. Maybe he was a good man, but maybe he wasn't. And who in their right mind rode out to the ranch in the middle of December?

When he walked into the house, his father glanced up. "What's wrong?"

"Rider headed this way," he said, making certain the rifle stood by the door.

"A visitor? Out here?" Minnie asked. She sat crocheting baby booties. Tiny socks to keep the baby's feet warm.

His thoughts exactly.

They were nearing the end of her pregnancy and Tripp didn't want to be too far from her.

What if it was the baby's father? Would he come all this way to find Minnie?

He tied his horse to the hitching post and then walked through the snow.

The man's boots walked up the porch and Tripp opened the door and gazed at him suspiciously.

"I'm here to see Beth," he said, his voice deep.

"Who are you?" Tripp asked. Everyone in town knew she was dead. Who was this man?

"Geoffrey Beau Hagan," the man said, holding out his hand.

Tripp lunged for him. The son of a bitch was the man who got his sister pregnant and then left. His fist smashed into the man's nose before he had a chance to defend himself.

His left hand came around and hit his cheek as he pummeled him.

"Stop, son. Stop right this moment," his father called.

But Tripp didn't want to stop beating the man. Because of him, Beth was dead.

Finally, the man's hand came up and grabbed his fist and held him.

"I don't know what caused you to want to fight me."

"You know damn well why," Tripp said. "You left her pregnant."

The man's jaw dropped and he licked his lips. "Honest. I didn't know."

He genuinely seemed stunned, and for a moment, Tripp hesitated though his instincts said keep fighting.

"Tripp, back off. Let the man come in and tell us what he knows."

Defeated, Tripp backed away. Nothing was going to bring Beth back, but still it felt good to get in a few licks before the man realized what he'd done.

He held out his hand to Pops, ignoring Tripp.

"Beau Hagan," he said.

"Loyd Maddox. And that ornery one is my son, Tripp, and his wife Minnie," Pops said. "Have a seat.

"Where's Beth?" he asked. "She's waited a long time for me to return. I want to ask for her hand in marriage."

"You've been gone almost two years," Tripp replied.

"Yes, the military sent me on a second job. I was supposed to be back last summer."

Tripp remembered her saying that everything would be all right come summer. He thought she was talking about the baby, but she'd been talking about Beau.

His father sighed. "Beth died in childbirth over a year ago."

For a few moments, the man sat there in shock. The man's head hung, and a tear slipped down his cheek. "I've been trying to get back, but the military refused every request for leave."

Minnie shook her head. Tripp could see she was moved by his story. "Did you love, Beth," she asked.

He turned to face her. "Yes, more than anything. Now she's gone forever. It had to be my baby. My child."

He covered his face with his hands. "Honest. I loved her. She didn't tell me she was expecting. We... joined the night before I had to leave for California. I promised her I would return in the summer. But the army had plans I didn't count on."

He raised his head. "Where's the child?"

"The baby died with her," Tripp said, suddenly feeling sorry for this man. To travel all this way with the intention of marrying his sister only to learn of her death.

Tripp could see his father's face had turn gray. The man

missed Beth badly. "It was a terrible delivery. The baby was breach and when he was born, the umbilical cord was wrapped around his neck. Beth hemorrhaged to death. That night, we lost them both."

At three o'clock in the morning, the doctor had come out of her room and told them she was gone. All the joy and excitement of a baby arriving, dissipated, not to mention dear sweet, Beth.

There was silence in the room as the heaviness hung at the loss of Beth.

"Answer a couple of questions for me," Pops said, gazing at the man in his long coat and Stetson hat that he now held in his hand.

The man's face was streaked with tears, pale from learning he'd lost not only his love but a child.

"Did you love my daughter, and would you have married her?"

"Most definitely," the man said without hesitation. Without even having to think about it.

With a sigh, Tripp realized that his sister's situation was not like Minnie's. His sister's man had truly loved her and their child. Only, fate had intervened and kept them apart. Clearly the man was upset.

"What do I do now?" he asked. "For two years, her sweet smile and laughter have kept me going. Knowing that soon I would return for her and we would marry. And a child. Dear God, we had a child and I never got a chance to see the baby."

"A little boy," Tripp said. "She named him Beau and now I understand why."

The man's shoulders shook with sobs at the realization of how the woman he loved had died along with his son. Fear gripped Tripp as he thought about Minnie. The baby was due in the next two weeks. What if something happened to her? What if this happened again?

Minnie rose and went into the bedroom. When she returned, she handed him one of the baby garments Beth had made in preparation for their child to be born.

"Beth made this for your son. Would you like to have it?"

He gazed down at the tiny shirt and sighed. "Thank you."

"Today when I left town, I was so excited to finally get to see her once again, but now I'm returning heart broken. Everything is lost. Tomorrow I was going to purchase land we'd been looking at. In my pocket is a ring I was going to propose with after I had spoken to you, Mr. Maddox. I couldn't wait to begin our life together. And now, I have nothing."

His father stood and walked to the man's side and patted him on the shoulder. "You have memories. Just like I have memories. While I can't say I was happy she was unmarried and pregnant. You've made me feel a lot better about her choice. She kept telling me, Pops, don't worry. Everything will be all right."

Tripp stood and offered the man his hand. "I'm sorry I reacted the way I did when I realized it was you."

The man stood and shook his hand. "Apology accepted. I must get going, so I reach town before dark." Tears welled up in his eyes. "I just can't believe she's gone."

"I know," Pops said. "I think I hear her voice all the time. Good luck to you, son."

"Thank you," he said and walked out the door.

After he was gone, they all sat around staring, sadness at the reality of how much of Beth's life he'd missed.

Finally Minnie stood. "Beth would not have wanted us to be sitting around moping like this. So get back to work. Both of you. But before you go, I have one thing to say. My baby's birth will not be like Beth's. I'm just putting that out there right now. It will be joyous because we've already gone through the hard part."

Tripp shook his head at his wife and smiled. She was talking to him. She was trying to ease his fears and he was grateful to her, but that didn't make them go away. Terror still gripped him at the thought of losing Minnie.

"Now, let's finish decorating for Christmas. We are going to have a good Christmas this year," Minnie said in a voice that demanded they all be happy.

Pops stood and smiled. "Damn girl, you get more bossy every day."

"I'm pregnant. Of course, I'm bossy."

CHAPTER 20

Two days before Christmas, Tripp went into town alone. Minnie was barely moving. The baby felt like it was sitting right in her lap. Though she put on a brave face for Pops and Tripp, the delivery concerned her. Frightened her to no end.

But she refused to give into her fears. Women had been having babies for thousands of years. She would live to see her baby. She refused to die, though she knew if it was her time, there was nothing she could do.

Still, she wanted her baby to live. She wanted to watch her grow into a woman. She wanted to live to make certain no man ever harmed her the way she'd been harmed.

And as her mother, she would believe her.

Yesterday, she had used all her material and asked Tripp to get her more when he went into town. Right now, Pops was cooking the meals and letting her rest.

The delivery had to be soon as she didn't know how she could grow any bigger. No longer could she see her feet, her dresses rode on top of her belly and her hips felt as wide as a door.

She was ready to hold her child.

While Tripp was out, she had knitted him some socks as a Christmas gift. What else could she do? Right now, riding into town seemed out of the question.

When the wagon rolled back into the yard, she felt relief that he made it home. She didn't like him being far from her. When the time came, she wanted him by her side.

There had not been any more snow and they expected a storm any day. They were overdue.

Tripp walked into the house and gazed at her. "You feeling okay?"

"Yes," she said, thinking she was ready for this to be over.

Walking to her, he gazed at her, his sky-blue eyes staring at her in a strange way. Like he was upset.

"Here is the material," he said. "That's all the baby flannel the mercantile in town had."

"That's perfect. Soon, I'll start making summer clothes."

He nodded, not responding.

"There's something else. A letter was received for Minnie Ravenel. They were holding it. Here it is."

She frowned and took the envelope from him. As she gazed at the handwriting, shock roiled through her.

No.

Why would he be writing to her?

Not trying to hide the letter, she slit it open.

Dear Minnie,

I made a lot of mistakes and I'm sorry. The only reason I was going to marry Jessica was because my family needed the money, so I started courting her. I spoke to your mother. Please come home to me. I want us to make a family with the baby. I love you and our child.

Come home,

Richard.

She looked at the address on the envelope. This had to be a joke. He didn't want her. He didn't want the baby. His family certainly didn't want her, not like Pops.

While the thought of home was pleasant. The memories were not. When she left, she'd been in shock. It wasn't until she reached Angel Creek that reality had set in. And even then, it was not good until she met Tripp.

Charleston and Richard weren't what she wanted. Sure, she missed her little sister and even her mother, but she didn't miss Charleston society.

The mountains of Montana, the snow, the sound of the coyotes howling at night, but most of all, Tripp was where she belonged.

She loved her husband and his attitude toward this child, and the way he showed her that she was important to him. No, he had not said the word *love* and she kept waiting for him to say it.

But so far, he had not spoken what she needed to hear. But that didn't mean she was going home to a man who treated her with no respect. Next week, he'd find someone else's life to ruin.

Her husband seemed agitated and she wondered if he worried about the letter. She had been here nearly two months. There was no returning to Charleston.

In that time, he'd shown her what real love was and what she had with Richard was nothing compared to what Tripp had shown her.

In fact, the thought of Richard was nauseating. Disgusting.

"Letter from home?"

"No," she said, laughing so hard, tears came in her eyes. "Richard. He wants me to come home."

Without a word, Tripp turned and walked out of the room. When he left the house, he slammed the door.

The man was angry. He hadn't asked her if she was going, just walked out the door assuming the worse. If he loved her, wouldn't he trust her?

Not exactly the thing you did to a pregnant woman in the last stages with her emotions all over the map. Especially the bad ones.

CHAPTER 21

Tripp walked out to put up the wagon and horses. He had been tempted not to give her the letter. Now it appeared that she was excited to receive a missive from the man who forced her to have sex with him.

He understood the man was the baby's father, but for Minnie to consider going back to him, he was shocked.

Maybe he was overreacting, but he expected her to tear up the letter with disgust and all she'd done was take it from him, read it, laughed with excitement and tears in her eyes.

Didn't she know how much it hurt him for her to even consider returning home to this monster?

The baby she carried he considered his own and he loved Minnie. He'd fallen in love with her as she brought joy and excitement into their home.

She'd insisted on a Christmas tree. Decorating it and even wrapping tiny presents and putting them under the tree. One for him, Pops, and the baby.

As he brushed the horse, his father came into the barn.

"You're upset."

"Damn right, I am," he said. "How can she consider going back to that man?"

"I don't think she is," his father said. "She read the letter and put it down. She even laughed like he's an idiot for even considering she would come home."

Tripp shook his head. "No, she laughed with happiness. She's going back to him."

His father took a deep breath, shaking his head. "You are just as stubborn as your mother. That girl in there is in love with you. Have you told her your feelings?"

Tripp didn't say anything. He'd planned to tell her Christmas Day when he gave her the wedding ring. It wasn't that he doubted his feelings, oh no, he was certain of how he felt about his wife. What he wasn't certain of were her feelings.

Was she just using him to give her child a name? Or did she have real emotions for him.

"I'm not saying anything until I'm certain she is in love with me, and right now, I think there's a man in Charleston that she loves. A man who forced himself on her."

Tripp was trembling with anger. He wanted to punch Richard's face for taking advantage of Minnie, and now disrupting their happiness just when the baby was about to be born.

"This girl is a real society, city girl, who has crossed the country to start a new life. She is learning to cook, to clean a house, and make baby clothes. She's doing everything she can to no longer be that rich, little spoiled girl. Can't you see that?"

It was one of the things he admired the most about her. She had been totally uprooted and came to Montana on a

MINNIE

wish and a prayer. And he thanked God every day he'd seen her step off that stagecoach. But, now, his worst nightmare was playing out.

She was leaving him to return to South Carolina to a man who would not love and appreciate her like he did.

"Yes, I see it. But, Pops, I think she still loves him."

After everything, her heart still belonged to the baby's father and that crushed Tripp.

"What makes you think that?"

"The way she smiled when she received the letter."

"A woman's smile can be a tricky thing. Sometimes it means they're happy and sometimes it's get the hell out of my way or you're a dead man. I believe that was a dead man's smile."

Tripp laughed. His father was thinking about their mother and he could see clearly that second smile. The one she used on her husband and children. Was that the type of smile Minnie gave him? Was he just overreacting because he was so scared of losing her?

"Son, the way to a good marriage is talking about things that bother you. Tell her your feelings."

He turned and glared at his father. "How can I? She's nine months pregnant. The woman can barely walk."

"Don't care. And yes, she's a mite emotional right now. But still you need to talk to her about your feelings."

"After the baby is born," he said, knowing she couldn't go anywhere right now.

His father started laughing. "All you're going to be doing once that baby arrives is feeding, changing, walking the floor with a crying kid, thinking you were crazy for agreeing to do this. And then the first time that child looks up and recognizes you and smiles, you'd do it again in a heartbeat."

The old man was not giving up the idea of him needing to talk to her. And he was probably right, but Tripp wasn't ready to talk just yet.

"Not now," he said, knowing he would do more harm than good if the talked to her at the moment.

His father sighed. "You're your mother's son. Supper is ready. Come in when you're ready," Pops said and walked out the door.

Tripp needed a few more minutes. More than anything, he wanted a life with Minnie and this child and eventually their own children.

At first, he'd only been attracted to her, but now, now he loved her so much, he couldn't imagine a day without her.

With one last stroke to the horse, he gave her a bag of oats and then headed to the house.

CHAPTER 22

It was Christmas Eve and Minnie had awoken this morning with a low back ache. Last night, exhausted, she went to bed right after supper. Her eyes had refused to cooperate and would not stay open.

But today, she jumped out of bed, eager to start preparing the Christmas meal. She wanted to bake a pumpkin pie and even make rolls, if she didn't give out. For tomorrow, the turkey was being cooked by Pops along with dressing.

She couldn't wait to let Tripp open his presents. One thing she'd made for him was a plaque with their name and wedding date. She'd also knitted him a scarf and a couple of pairs of socks.

No, they were not big items, but they were made with love. Because she loved this man dearly.

After she got up, she went to use the chamber pot in a closet that Tripp had made for them to use. It was nice and private and the further along she was, the more she had to use it.

When she returned to the bedroom, Tripp was awake.

"Merry Christmas Eve," she told him excited about the day.

"Good morning," he said, rising in bed. He watched her as she dressed for the day. "We need to talk."

That sounded ominous and today was Christmas Eve. Their first Christmas and she wanted it to be joyful.

"All right. What about?"

Tripp shook his head and then he glared at her. "When are you going home to Richard?"

Stunned, she jerked and glanced at him. "What are you talking about? I'm not going home to that louse."

Why in the world would he think she was returning to Charleston and Richard?

"But you laughed when you read his letter."

"Yes, I did, because it was such bullshit. Pardon my language."

"What do you mean?"

Now she could feel her rage starting to build. The man actually believed she would leave him and the life they were creating to return to a man who forced her to have sex with him.

Who was the reason she was pregnant? Who was going to marry another woman after promising himself to her?

"Do you trust me?" she asked, her hands on her hips.

She was nine months pregnant and he thought she would catch the next stage?

"Of course," he replied.

"Then why don't you show it? Yesterday, I thought the man an idiot to write to tell me he loves me and wants me to come home, when he wouldn't even speak to me when I lived in Charleston. I actually wondered if the letter was a prank."

"But you smiled and laughed and I thought you were happy to hear from him."

That made her even angrier. She was about to give birth and Tripp had not even said he loved her. What was wrong with men? Did they just like to get women with child and not think about their feelings?

"Just because I smile and laugh does not mean I want anything else to do with that man. It meant I thought he was a complete fool for sending me a letter begging my forgiveness when I would just as soon light a match to his lying ass. He means nothing to me. Do you understand now?"

"Yes," he said softly. "You don't normally get this upset. Are you feeling all right?"

She was enraged. All this time she believed that Tripp knew her feelings for him. She was waiting on him to tell her he loved her before she confessed her feelings. And instead, he didn't trust her.

"No, I'm nine months pregnant. My back aches, my feet hurt, my breasts hurt, and this baby is kicking me in the bladder. Plus, my husband thinks I want to go back to Charleston to a man I despise. So my perfect Christmas Eve morning is not starting off too well."

Tripp threw back the covers and began to put his pants on. "I'm sorry."

She didn't know how to respond. "Don't ask me about Richard again. As far as I'm concerned, he's dead."

With that she shuffled out of the bedroom. Tears pricked her eyes and she would have loved to have had a long conversation with a woman about pregnancy. Her mother especially. But she was thousands of miles away.

When would it end, and her emotions stop feeling like a volcano resided inside her?

Right now, she was so angry, she just wanted to leave. Get away from both men. She thought about Ginger.

She had just gone through this same ordeal. She would know how she was feeling. Maybe it was a small thing, and she was making it larger, but right now, she was so angry, she wanted to kick and scream.

Why? Pregnancy was making her crazy. Right now, nothing felt normal. Nothing. And she was starting to hate everything about the life she was creating.

As soon as Tripp left, she would hitch the wagon and go to town. It was an hour there and an hour back. She'd be home before he came in from the fields.

At this moment, she just needed some time alone. Some time away from everything and everyone who didn't understand what being pregnant felt like.

Her biggest concern was could she get in and out of the wagon by herself without falling.

Pops usually liked to lie down for an afternoon nap. Once he fell asleep, she was going to town. It had been months since she'd been there.

She needed another woman's advice and assurance everything would be all right. Were all men like Richard and Tripp? How did pregnancy affect other women's bodies, and would this baby ever come or would she remain pregnant the rest of her life?

CHAPTER 23

Twice Minnie almost backed out of leaving and going into town. Her back had been aching all day, but she knew that was typical pregnancy pains. All she felt was irritated and hurt and angry.

She loved Tripp, but he had not said the words and yet he dared to accuse her of returning to Richard. That would never happen.

It took her thirty minutes to hitch the wagon. Only because she had to keep stopping and resting. Then it took her another five minutes to climb up in the wagon. Wherever she stopped, she would need to see if someone could help her climb in again.

Once she was in the wagon, she wrapped the lap robe around her. The clouds were beginning to gather in the west, so she would need to make this quick. With a click to the horses, they pulled out of the barn and onto the drive and then the road.

With a sigh, she tried to relax. It felt good to be out of the house. To anticipate seeing people again.

She urged the horses to hurry, but then she bounced so much on the wagon seat, she had to slow them down. Her back was really starting to hurt and she wondered if she had made a mistake in going to town.

On the outskirts of Angel Creek, she felt warm liquid gush between her legs. Oh no, her water had just broken. Fear gripped her chest. She was going into labor.

What did she do now?

She drove to the livery stable and spoke to the man there. "I'd like to leave my wagon and horses here for a little while."

They arranged payment and he took the wagon.

The only person she knew in town was Ginger. As she walked along the sidewalk, she had a contraction, her wet skirt clinging to her cold legs. The pain was sharp and swift, and she paused and waited for it to pass.

The sun was beginning to set. It had taken her a lot longer to get here. She prayed that Tripp would find her. Why had she thought this was a good idea? Tears were on the edge of her lashes and she realized she had done something completely crazy.

No nine-month pregnant woman should be traveling by herself.

She pounded on Ginger's door. Nothing. No one was home.

The doctor was right around the corner. She had to reach the doctor.

She walked around the corner to the doctor's office and pounded on his door. No answer.

Where was everyone? It was Christmas Eve. Shouldn't they be home?

Crying, she walked to the hotel. She would get a room for the night.

On her way there, a contraction hit her. Crying out, she leaned against a building and waited for the pain to subside.

She walked into the Angel Creek Hotel. They were having a big party with lots of the minors celebrating Christmas.

"Do you have any rooms?" she asked.

"No, ma'am, we're sold out for the night."

Tearfully, she turned and walked out the door. She rubbed her hand on her belly.

"I'm so sorry, baby. I've made a horrible decision. You've got to hold on. I'll get the horse and we'll go home. Just please don't come until I get home. Please."

Pain gripped her and she had to lean against a building wall.

"Please. Wait."

How many mothers begged their babies not to come just yet?

By now it was dark, and she knew she was in serious trouble. But no matter what, she had to get home.

She went into the livery and they had closed for the day. Looking around, she cried out as another pain hit her. They were coming closer and closer now.

"Help!"

No answer. She was truly alone. How many women were alone when they gave birth? She'd been so foolish to leave the house. What was she thinking?

Another pain knocked her to her knees, and she fell to the floor. As soon as the contraction passed, she found fresh hay and a clean blanket. She spread the blanket on the hay and then lay down. She removed her drawers and waited for the next contraction.

Tears spilled down her cheeks.

"Tripp, please find me. I'm sorry."

Just then another contraction hit her, and she screamed as the pain consumed her. They were coming faster and faster now. It wouldn't be long. And she would be alone when the baby came.

CHAPTER 24

Tripp raced down the road beside himself with worry. What had he done? This morning she had not been herself and he'd confronted her about Richard. Which, in looking back, he'd been stupid.

He let his fear override his common sense.

The woman was not going back to Charleston to a man who had disrespected her from the time they were courting.

When he should be supporting her, knowing she felt bad and was in the last days of her pregnancy, he'd caused her even more pain and worry.

As soon as Pops woke from his nap and realized she'd left, he found Tripp. Now he was on his way into town, thinking that's where she was headed. If not, then he didn't know where she'd gone.

As he rode into town, darkness overcame the small town. He looked around for the horses and wagon. Nothing. He went to Ginger's house since she was really the only person in town that Minnie knew, but quickly realized that tonight was the church Christmas party and they were busy celebrating.

It was Christmas Eve. One of the holiest nights of the year. The year of our Lord and Savior's birth.

He went to the church but didn't find her and saw the doctor at the party.

Next, he tried the hotel and the boy behind the counter told him she had been in earlier, but they had no available rooms.

Where could she be?

As he walked by the livery stable, he heard a scream.

Dragging through the snow, he ran across the street, bursting through the barn door.

"Minnie," he cried.

"Tripp. You came."

"Of course, I did."

She was breathing hard. "The baby. It's coming. It's time."

He glanced down. It was dark, he couldn't see anything.

"Hold on," he said. "I'm going to find a lantern."

"No, don't leave me," she cried.

"I'm not going far. We need light if you're having our baby."

She cried. "I kept telling the baby to wait, but she refused to listen to me. I'm sorry I left. But I had to talk to another woman."

He laughed as he searched the barn. Somehow he had to keep her from panicking. And he couldn't let her see how fearful he was. Of all places for them to have their first child.

"Did you find someone?"

"No, not even the doctor was at home."

He found a lantern, lit it, then carried it back to where she was lying on a pile of fresh hay.

"Here comes another one," she cried. Her body was opening, but what if she had trouble? What if she died just like Beth had died? What if he lost her? He couldn't live with himself. Not again.

"Breathe," he said. "Short little breaths."

She panted, her eyes wide with fright.

"I should get the doctor," he said, thinking he couldn't do this.

"No, don't you dare leave me," she said. "You can deliver this baby."

He had delivered horses and cattle. Could it be much different? Only this time it was from the woman he loved. And the child he wanted.

"Tripp, I have faith in you. You can deliver our baby."

Taking a deep breath, he went to find clean water in the barn. He found soap and water and cleaned his hands.

"Tripp," she screamed, "the baby is coming."

Running back to her, he gazed down at her.

"Don't you dare die on me," he said. "I love you and want to spend the rest of my days with you."

She gave a weak laugh. "You didn't have to say you love me during labor. It's all right if you don't love me."

Stunned, he stopped what he was doing, which was seeing how close the baby was to coming and gazed at her.

"I have loved you since the time I laid eyes on you. I was smitten the moment you stepped out of that stagecoach. Tomorrow, I had planned on telling you and giving you my mother's wedding ring. You see, I wanted to make it a big deal."

She reached out and touched his forehead. "I'm sorry. I kind of messed that up."

"Yes, you did, but that's okay. How about instead we have a baby?"

She smiled. "Do you realize the importance of this day? Of where we are?"

He grinned. "Yeah, it's kind of surreal. The night our savior was born in a barn and Mary, his mother, put him in a manger."

"Yes," she said, tears filling her eyes.

"Promise me, you will not do this with our next child."

A chuckle escaped her and then it changed as she began to push. Her face turning red. "The baby is coming."

He glanced between her legs and saw the most amazing sight. The crowning of a tiny head. Tears filled his eyes as he watched his first child enter this world.

First, the head slipped out and then he helped the shoulders and then the rest of the slimy body fell into his hands.

"A girl. Honey, we have a girl."

He wiped her face clean so she could breathe and she let out a squeal loud enough to have the horses in a stall over making nervous noises.

His training kicked in and he quickly delivered the afterbirth and cut the umbilical cord, tying it off.

Then he took off his shirt, wrapped his daughter in it and handed her to her mother.

"Oh, look at her. She's so perfect," Minnie said crying.

Relief filled him as his hands began to shake. No, this was not another tragedy, but rather a joyous occasion as they celebrated the birth of their first born.

"Have you picked out a name?"

"Yes," she said, smiling through her tears. "Beth. Our first daughter will be named Beth."

Tripp lay down beside his wife on the hay and they gazed at their baby girl. "Thank you. I love you."

"You make my life complete. I love you," Minnie said. "No other man will ever take me from you. You have my heart."

Tripp kissed his wife and their baby girl squeaked as she opened her eyes and gazed at her parents.

"Welcome to the world, Beth."

CHAPTER 25

Christmas Eve, 1888
"And that, dear daughter, is how your father brought you into this world."

The retelling of the story filled her with such love for her husband. Since that fateful night, they had lost Pops and had one miscarriage, but other than that, their lives were filled with joy and love.

"Oh, Mama, you were such a brave young woman," she said. "To travel across the country, pregnant."

"But look how God rewarded me. Not only do I have a beautiful daughter, but a husband who has brought me nothing but joy and happiness."

"And five more children," Beth said.

Actually six Minnie thought of the one they lost. Her heart ached when she remembered him but knew he was an angel in heaven.

"Yes, indeed. And I love all of you. But you, dear daughter, have a special place in our heart. Because you brought us together."

"I love you, Mama," Beth said, snuggling down in the covers.

"Are you curious about the man who created you?"

All these years later and Minnie still had a hard time saying the man's name. Years ago, she'd let go of the hate she felt for him and concentrated on the goodness in her life.

Her daughter's face twisted, and she shook her head. "Not really. He doesn't sound like a good man. My real father is a man that all of his children look up to."

Minnie felt tears well up in her eyes. This was what she loved about this child. Her way of seeing the world.

She learned so much from her daughter.

"It's all right if you ever want to meet him. You could have half brothers and sisters."

"No, I don't think so. It's better to let sleeping dogs lie."

Her words filled Minnie with happiness and yet it would be all right if she ever wanted to see him.

"Can you sleep now?"

"Yes," Beth said. "Tell Papa that someday I hope I find a man just like him to marry."

It was all she could do to keep the tears from falling onto her daughter's face.

"I will, love, now rest. Tomorrow is a big day."

Minnie walked out of the bedroom and into the room she shared with Tripp.

"Is she all right?"

"Hold me," she said as she crawled into bed with the man she had married eighteen years ago. "She's fine. Wise beyond her years."

She told Tripp what Beth had said about him and he held onto her tightly.

"We are so blessed."

"Remember that night eighteen years ago? Two young people trying to figure out their relationship, in a stable…"

"Delivering our daughter on Christmas Eve in a barn."

Minnie glanced at her husband. "Thank you for the wonderful life you've given me and our children."

"I love you more today than I did on that Christmas Eve," he said.

"My prayer is that all of our children will be as blessed in love as we have been."

"Merry Christmas, Minnie."

"Merry Christmas, Tripp."

THANK YOU FOR READING MINNIE. Oh, I hope you enjoyed this story as much as I enjoyed writing it. When we decided to do another set of Angel Creek Christmas Brides, I knew I wanted to write a story about a young, pregnant woman crossing the country and then being rejected. Of course, I knew she would receive her happily ever after. Minnie and Tripp were a great couple. Please be sure to leave a review! Continue reading to learn about the next bride brought to you by Cynthia Woolf.

ADELE JENSEN GAVE her heart to the wrong man. After ten years as mistress to a power-hungry and vengeful man, she realizes her mistake and leaves New York behind to start a new life in Montana as a mail-order bride. Afraid her new husband won't approve of her past, she creates a new identity for herself. She hopes with all her heart her new husband will be the loving husband and father she's always dreamed of. But can she keep her secret from her new husband or will her dreams be destroyed forever?

Edward Wharton doesn't trust women. In fact, the only female he wants to take care of is his seven year old daughter whose mother left him for a gambler and a fifth of whiskey and life in the saloon. When a stagecoach accident took her life, he couldn't find it in his heart to mourn her death, nor to forgive her treachery. But his little girl needs a mother, and Edward is tired of battling life alone. A mail order bride seems to be the perfect solution to his dilemma, he needs a woman in his life, but not in his bed. Definitely not in his heart.

Richard Douglas keeps what's his, and as far as he's concerned, that includes his runaway mistress, Adele. She defied him. Ran from him. Made demands she had no right to make. And he will have her back, no matter the cost.

Angel Creek, Montana is a wild frontier where only the strong survive. Richard's arrival will test Edward's resolve not to love again. Will Adele find the courage to conquer her past and Edward's untamed heart?

PLEASE LEAVE A REVIEW

Did you enjoy the book? Reviews help authors. I would appreciate you posting a review.

Follow Sylvia McDaniel on Facebook.

Sign up for my New Book Alert at www. SylviaMcDaniel.com and receive a complimentary book.

After the war leaves Charleston devastated, and with few prospects of marriage, five friends headed west for a new life and a possible love match. A year later, they invite six friends to join them. The following Christmas, they're still homesick and in desperate need of a deeper connection with their old life, so what else can a Southern Belle do but invite more would-be brides to travel west?

Angel Creek is about to be invaded yet again by more Southern Misses and the town most definitely will never be the same!

CHRISTMAS 2018 BOOKS
Book 1: Charity — Sylvia McDaniel
Book 2: Julia — Lily Graison
Book 3: Ruby — Hildie McQueen
Book 4: Sarah — Peggy McKenzie
Book 5: Anna — Everly West

CHRISTMAS 2019 BOOKS
Book 6: Caroline — Lily Graison
Book 7: Melody — Caroline Clemmons
Book 8: Elizabeth — Jo Grafford
Book 9: Emma — Peggy McKenzie
Book 10: Viola — Cyndi Raye
Book 11: Ginger — Sylvia McDaniel

CHRISTMAS 2020 BOOKS
Book 12: Abigail — Peggy McKenzie
Book 13: Grace — Jo Grafford
Book 14: Pearl — Hildie McQueen
Book 15: Rebecca — Lily Graison
Book 16: Charlotte — Kari Trumbo
Book 17: Minnie — Sylvia McDaniel
Book 18: Adele — Cynthia Woolf
Book 19: Victoria — Maxine Douglas
Book 20: Meg — Caroline Clemmons

CHRISTMAS 2021 BOOKS
Book 21: Glenda — Hildie McQueen
Book 22: Temperance — Lily Graison
Book 23: Lilly — Jo Grafford
Book 24: Hannah — Peggy McKenzie
Book 25: Amy — Caroline Clemmons
Book 26: Cora — Sylvia McDaniel

Also By Sylvia McDaniel
Western Historicals
A Hero's Heart
Second Chance Cowboy
Ethan

American Brides
**Katie: Bride of Virginia

Angel Creek Christmas Brides
**Charity
**Ginger
**Minne
**Cora

Bad Girls of the West
Scandalous Sadie
Ravenous Rose
Tempting Tessa
Nellie's Redemption

The Burnett Brides Series
The Rancher Takes A Bride
The Outlaw Takes A Bride
The Marshal Takes A Bride
The Christmas Bride
Boxed Set

Lipstick and Lead Series
Desperate

ALSO BY

Deadly
Dangerous
Daring
**Determined
Deceived
Defiant
Devious
Lipstick and Lead Box Set Books 1-4
Lipstick and Lead Box Set Books 5-9
Lipstick and Lead Box Set Books 1-9
**Quinlan's Quest

Mail Order Bride Tales
**A Brother's Betrayal
**Pearl
**Ace's Bride

Scandalous Suffragettes of the West
**Abigail
Bella
Mistletoe Scandal

Southern Historical Romance
A Scarlet Bride

The Cuvier Women
Wronged
Betrayed
Beguiled
Boxed Set

ALSO BY

The Debutante's of Durango
The Debutante's Scandal
The Debutante's Gamble
The Debutante's Revenge
The Debutante's Santa

** Denotes a sweet book.

Want to learn about my new releases before anyone else? Sign up for my New Book Alert and receive a complimentary book.

USA Today Best-selling author, Sylvia McDaniel obviously has too much time on her hands. With over fifty western historical and contemporary romance novels, she spends most days torturing her characters. Bad boys deserve punishment and even good girls get into trouble. Always looking for the next plot twist, she's known for her sweet, funny, family-oriented romances.

Married to her best friend for over twenty-five years, they recently moved to the state of Colorado where they like to hike, and enjoy the beauty of the forest behind their home with their spoiled dachshund Zeus. (He has his own column in her newsletter.)

Their grown son, still lives in Texas. An avid football watcher, she loves the Broncos and the Cowboys, especially when they're winning.

www.SylviaMcDaniel.com
Sylvia@SylviaMcDaniel.com
The End!

Made in the USA
Middletown, DE
10 November 2021